It Lasts Forever and Then It's Over

Anne de Marcken

It Lasts Forever
and Then It's Over

A NEW DIRECTIONS
PAPERBACK ORIGINAL

Published simultaneously by New Directions in the United States,
Fitzcarraldo in the United Kingdom, and Giramondo in Australia.

Manufactured in the United States of America
First published as a New Directions Paperbook in 2024

Library of Congress Cataloging-in-Publication Data
Names: De Marcken, Anne, author.
Title: It lasts forever and then it's over / Anne de Marcken.
Other titles: It lasts forever and then it is over
Description: First edition. | New York : New Directions Publishing, 2024.
Identifiers: LCCN 2023045508 | ISBN 9780811237857 (paperback) |
ISBN 9780811237864 (ebook)
Subjects: LCSH: Mortality—Fiction. | LCGFT: Novels.
Classification: LCC PS3604.E1289 I8 2024 | DDC 811/.6—dc23/eng/20231003
LC record available at https://lccn.loc.gov/2023045508

2 4 6 8 10 9 7 5 3

New Directions Books are published for James Laughlin
by New Directions Publishing Corporation
80 Eighth Avenue, New York 10011

for M

Without you, that indefinite, promiscuous, and expansive pronoun, we are wrecked and we fall.

—Judith Butler

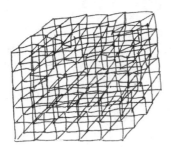

PART 1

We're stories telling stories, nothing.
—Fernando Pessoa

I LOST MY LEFT ARM today. It came off clean at the shoulder. Janice 2 picked it up and brought it back to the hotel. I would have thought it would affect my balance more than it has. It is like getting a haircut. The air moving differently around the remaining parts of me. Also by turns a sense of newness and lessness—free me, undead me, don't look at me.

Isn't it strange that I never knew a single living Janice and now I know three?

I stay in bed all day. If I lie on my right side, I can keep the arm balanced as if it is still part of me. Or I can pretend it is your arm and that you are in bed with me. I think about how we used to take a blanket into the dunes and wrap up together. Wake with sand in our hair and in the corners of our eyes. Sound of the ocean big as the sky. I miss sleep. I miss you.

—

Mitchem says I'm in denial. That I am depressed because I am indulging in a sense of loss instead of wonder. "Embrace your new existence," he says. I picture myself trying to do this with one arm.

When I was alive, I imagined something redemptive about the end of the world. I thought it would be a kind of purification. Or at least a simplification. Rectification through reduction. I could picture the empty cities, the reclaimed land.

That was the future. This is now.

The end of the world looks exactly the way you remember. Don't try to picture the apocalypse. Everything is the same.

Mitchem says it is important to do small, ordinary tasks when you're depressed. That even if I don't do anything else all day, I should make the bed. This morning he came in and opened the curtains. He stood over me, that half-moon head of his backlit by the window. He picked up the arm from where it was lying on the floor and held it out like something I needed to account for. He said, "You've experienced a significant loss." He said, "It isn't just your arm." He said, "You're grieving your life." Since he broke off his penis he's Mr. Wisdom. When he left, I closed the curtains again. A glow creeps under my room door from the hallway where the lights are always on.

Yesterday Mitchem preached in the lobby. Today he set up on the roof. He stands on a side table from one of the rooms. Afterward I saw Bob following him around wearing a rain poncho like the one Mitchem wears. Uh oh.

—

Tried to make a harness for the arm. It is too heavy. Dead weight. Ha ha.

Found a shirt today with cuffs that button. It is red. I stuffed in the arm and buttoned myself in with it. The fit isn't good. The arm slides down bare up to the elbow and flops forward in my way. Like the dislocated limb of a mannequin. It gets turned around in the sleeve and elbows me in the side. It is strange to see it like this. My hand. My wrist. The fingernails.

Smoke has settled down in the sound. Sunrises and sets have been dull and angry. The full moon dark red. Even inside the hotel it is hazy. Exit signs are dim irony at the ends of the long hallways. Wildfire, back-burn, blitz. Any way you look at it, a blaze we set.

Mitchem preached on the roof again tonight. Only the undead can truly understand the meaning of life, he said. There is no meaning, he said. Bob was there. He seems to have been promoted. Now he carries the side table around and stands nearby when Mitchem is up there. Which comes first, a believer or a religion? Others are showing up now, too. I can't describe how strange it is. Someone puts her hands up in the air and then the others do it. Someone moans, and the others moan. You can see how this will go. There is talk of a revival.

—

That's another thing—most of us can't remember who we are ... were ...are. We are character actors to ourselves—people we recognize but can't name.

It really bothers some of the hotel guests. They always have the troubled, distracted look of a person trying to remember something simple. They are attracted to one another. They sit together saying one name after another hoping if they hear their own name they will know it. They write names on the walls, in the elevator, on the air exchange unit on the roof, in the dust the dust the dust that covers everything. You can take a name for yourself. You can leave one for someone else. But why choose the name Janice when someone else is already using it? And who chooses the name Bob?

Carlos says that names are the most commonplace ritual. "Little prayers," he says, that connect us to each other and to humanity. He tells me a story: When he was a boy he had a favorite toy. A small truck. Like the truck on his family's farm. He kept it in his pocket all the time. It was metal with moving wheels made of hard black rubber and open spaces instead of a windshield and windows. It was green, but in many places the paint was worn off to dull grey metal. As he walked along, he would take the truck out of his pocket and drive it down the length of railings, on walls. He drove it along his own body—up his arm, across his face, loving the feel of the wheels. He made a system of roads in the flower patch behind his house. In secret he made a tiny paper version of himself that he put inside. He made up stories about where he was going. He put grass in the back and pretended he and his father were taking hay to the cattle the way they did in real life, but in his imagination he got to drive.

He was eight the year his brother was born and his mother died. He wrapped up the truck in a sock and buried it. For a long time he didn't remember the truck. He still doesn't remember where he buried it. But he knows it is there and so is the time before everything changed. He says this is how our names work.

"But your name isn't Carlos," I say.

"Carlos is the name I have given my name," he says.

"You seem like a Carlos," I say.

I haven't asked, but I think Marguerite is not Marguerite's real name. It is the kind of name you pick for French class. Mine was Genevieve. I remember that, but not my actual name. I don't miss my name and I haven't bothered to replace it. I miss your name. I'm sorry, but I have forgotten it, too. I don't look for it on the walls. The thought that I might read it and pass it by, just go on to the next name, is terrible. Like meeting you in another life and failing to recognize you.

Marguerite has grey hair that she wears in two long braids wrapped around her head in a kind of crown into which she has stuck things. Feathers. A pencil. Twist ties. A Barbie arm. I tell her about Anton and the original QB and the way you drove like your dad. She lets me go on and on. I think she is busy with her own ideas.

Some hotel guests are better storytellers than others. Some are funny. Some had more interesting lives. Remember their lives better than others. Make things up. Sometimes we get on a topic and just list things. First jobs. Home. Parents.

Food. A guest called Blake tells the same story over and over. It isn't even a story, really, about stealing a pack of grape bubblegum. Another called Alison remembers all the lines from *Moonstruck*.

Somebody tell a joke.

Is that man praying?

You'll eat it bloody to feed your blood.

Yesterday she said to me, "*Where's* my *hand? Where's* my *bride?*"

I worry that I am getting other guests' stories mixed up with my own. Did I like strawberry ice cream? Did I grow a zucchini the size of Ed's leg? Did I have a green toy truck?

If I ever remember your name, how will I know it was really your name?

I said that I found the red shirt. I mean that I took it off the body of a man I killed and ate. I don't tell you about the killing. The eating. I protect myself from what you will think. You who are dead.

My rule used to be that I would not eat what I was not willing to kill. I said to meat eaters, "If I get hungry enough, I might be willing to kill a cow." It was a pragmatic morality. Which is not morality. A naturopath told me that based on my blood type I ought to eat meat. What was her name? Well I'm a meat-eater now. And I could fill a book with what I didn't know about hunger.

In truth the rule had to do with the degree to which I was able to ignore the expression of an individual animal's will to live, which was directly related to how effectively that animal communicated to me both its individuality and its suffering. When I steamed a pot of little Manila clams, the indications of their existential crises—I think it is going too far to say fear—were generalized and inscrutable enough that I could overlook them. Conceal from myself the fact and ramifications of my actions.

I cared less for the man in the red shirt than a clam. It was strange, though, to undress him. Intimate. To unbutton the shirt. To take his arms from their sleeves. Like undressing a sleeping child. Awkward. Tender. His freckled skin. The hollow of his diaphragm. His nipples. There was a purple scar on the inside of one arm—long and thin like the burn I once got from a curling iron.

I don't like to use the word flesh because it sounds too essential or universal. Like he and I are part of something bigger—actors in roles originated in dark prehistory and that will be inherited and inhabited by other actors. Neither the actor nor the role quite whole or answerable for any actions. That is what ritual does. It excuses us. Comforts us. Places us in a context so vast and ineffable we can confuse it with truth because it is impersonal and because it has a lineage and because it extends all the way—but only—to the limits of what we can conceive.

Better to say I ate his leg but left his foot. His bones were pinkish blue.

Marguerite, Carlos and I went swimming in the sound today. Wading, really, but all the way in. We can walk right in and under. I had dreams of this when I was a kid, that I was walking around on the bottom and breathing in the ocean like it was thick air. It is the jellyfish time. They pulsed around us like a galaxy of pale, daytime moons. Maybe Mitchem is right about beauty. He says it persists because it was one of the few real things. Beauty. Dreams. Boredom. Hunger. More than anything, hunger.

Perhaps the chief difference between me now and me then is my tolerance for terror. I think this has to be related to the abstraction of pain. Physical pain. Emotional pain. The pain of others. My own. The flinch is there still. And I think the pain itself is there somewhere. But it is locked up. Locked up in a tiny, invisible, apocalypse-proof kernel. The tiny translucent egg of a subatomic insect laid at the center of each of us. When we're gone, if we're ever gone, this is what will remain of us. Fossilized pain. Not carbon. There will be a pain stratum where all the pain will settle. Pain shale. Pain veins. Quartzy ligatures made of tears, sighs, sobs, moans, terrible screams. Maybe when there are no more living, pain will have real value. Pain inflation will drive a pain market. There will be pain panners like gold panners, shaking out the suffering. Pain frackers. Pain centrifuges. We will build a giant pain collider to crack open its secret structure and release the tiny, lace-winged gasp of our lost humanity. Humanity. That word.

Maybe we kill the living to get at their pain. Or our own.

I was thinking about golems. I was thinking that I am like a golem. I feel more like earth now than like an animal. Mud and sticks and rags that look and act something like a live thing. And I thought: But really I'm more like an owl pellet. A boney, furry, coughed-up turd that walks and talks.

But then it wasn't just a joke to myself. It became an idea. A middle-of-the-night idea. All my ideas now are middle-of-the-night ideas. Perfectly lucid and perfectly flawed. I am having a very long sleepless night. Exactly the opposite of the endless sleep that is death. I had the idea that I'd make myself a new arm. An owl pellet arm. Mud and hair. I pretended to wake you up and tell you. I said out loud: "Don't let me forget — owl pellets."

I've already told you this story, but I'll tell you again. When I was little and my mom was working at the corral, I spent all day as a horse. I ate molasses covered oats from the grain bin. I drank from the water troughs. When I ran I was galloping. I'd look along the edge of the forest for two sticks just the right length and hold them in my hands for front legs. The sticks helped me see myself, feel myself, as a horse. It is my human shape that allows me to see myself, feel myself, as a human. Without the arm, it is that much harder. If you were here, you would tell me that you would have fallen in love with me no matter when we met. Even when I was a horse, you would say. Even now, you would say. Even now you would fall in love with me.

I miss the way we retold each other the same stories as if we'd just remembered them. And the way we'd play along, asking questions to get at the details we already knew. I think it was so we would still recognize each other even as we changed. Like a snake is the same snake even after shedding its old skin. But now we are just the stories. You. Me. All of us. Just the raspy husk of ourselves. Mitchem says this is another way we're superior—because we are, at the same time, creator and creation.

It is not precisely accurate to say that nothing has changed. It's all farther along. And it is quieter. And the quiet is emptier. At night, walking the streets, it is especially noticeable. You can hear things settling, the way an old house settles. Creaking and popping. Some buildings are tilting into the fill on which they were built. Walls buckle. Doors get wedged shut. Sometimes a window will suddenly crack. That bone on bone sound. Or the glass falls out of its frame. You notice eventually that the hollow look of the storefronts is due to the fact their windows have all broken out. In places, the layers of asphalt have split and slipped to reveal the old brick pavement. It makes me nostalgic for something I never knew.

Also, the moon is always full.

So I went down to the waterfront with the arm and I was sitting with it on the thin strip of beach between the water and the grass where the geese graze and poop. A dog shows up and sniffs around the arm. Then he does the dog thing—goes weak in the shoulder and starts rolling on the arm. I am so outraged. I stand up and I yell at him. I pick up the arm and hit him with it and I'm yelling, "Bad dog. No. No." Ridiculous. "Get out of here. Go home." Dead serious even though

I'm holding my arm like it's a salami and pointing it at him. And he has that look on his face—ashamed of his weakness but determined to do it again if he gets the chance. It's the smell, I suppose. Irresistible.

Which raises the question of decomposition. And the bigger question of what and how consolidated or generally distributed is my animating force. Has the part of me that was associated with my arm died? Will it also decompose? Why is my arm dead while I am undead?

On my way back to the hotel, I found a dead crow in the street.

There is more to say about the crow, but I don't know how to say it. I don't know why it is hard. Like a confession. How do you confess? I kept the crow. I have it now. I wanted it. Not to eat. But terribly. I wanted it. Not sexually, but like that. It was that powerful. And terrible-seeming. The moment you realize you want something that is not yours. The moment you let yourself have it. I took it to my room and lay down on top of it, the crow. I just lay there with it under my chest. If I were living, my heart would have been pounding right where the crow was pressed between me and the carpet. I keep thinking about its black feathers. Its thin legs and clenched feet. I'm thinking about them now. I want to hold the crow in both hands and I only have the one and that seems like the whole truth of everything.

—

Today we burned the arm. We lashed together a raft and set it on there. We put Janice 2's pinkie on too. In a little tinder nest. We set fire to them at dusk and shoved them off into the sound like heroes. Goodbye arm. Goodbye pinkie. Mitchem said a few words for the departed. We disagree about ritual. He says ritual is fundamental. I don't ask what he did to honor the memory of his penis.

Afterward I pretend-smoked one of Carlos's cigarettes. I used to smoke a Bic pen waiting for the school bus on cold mornings. Then I pretended my breath was smoke. Now I pretend my breath is breath.

I carved out a space for the crow. Inside. Up under my ribs. I wrapped it in a sleeve of the red shirt and put it up in there. Little red mummy. I have a crow inside me and no one can know. I can feel it all the time. It is like the entire night sky and all the stars and every beautiful sound you can imagine. It is like being too excited to sleep. It is like being twelve years old and stripping off my clothes outside in the rain. Savage. Girl. Suddenly awake to the deviance available in every ordinary moment. The possibilities of my current situation had not occurred to me before now. The freedom. There is a crow in my chest.

PART 2

For me there are two alternatives: either swallow or break free.
—Susan Howe

THERE IS A BLACK FEATHERED thing inside of me. It's as if all my life I wanted it there. Or the space for it was there. The possibility.

Ideas of things, feelings of things, are becoming the things themselves. When I look up at the moon, I expect it to turn toward me and speak. Every metaphor presents itself as what was there all along.

I might have described the feeling in my chest as a crow. Now the feeling is the thing. A furled, feathered thing rotting into my unrotting flesh.

A hotel might once have been a metaphor for the body, for purgatory, for any transitory site. Muffled hallways. The repeating pattern of low-pile carpet. Sconce lighting. Echoing emergency stairwells that smell vaguely familiar. The sound of doors closing. Plastic ice buckets. Theft-proof hangers without hooks. Drawers no one ever uses. Perfect. And now here we actually are, none of us sure when we checked in or whether this is really our luggage.

And of course us. Zombies used to be drug addicts, television watchers, videogame players. Now zombies are zombies. Consumers are consumers.

There is a shift and there is the sound it makes. *Shift*. The sound of a necessary adjustment, of a thing pushed into place.

I have to stop myself from constantly reaching up inside my shirt to check that the crow is still there, still hidden.

I decide I will bind up my chest to hold it in. With the help of a pair of nail scissors borrowed from the overnight case in Janice 2's room, and solving a series of problems, I make a sizable pile of bandaging out of the top sheet from the second bed in my room before realizing that this good idea is impossible with only one arm.

I find Marguerite on the roof. "I need your help," I say. We go back to my room.

She doesn't seem surprised and doesn't ask any questions. She presses the loose end of a sheet bandage to my sternum. "Hold this here," she says. I do as I'm told and she wraps me up, one strip after another, binding me snuggly, flattening out my breasts. It feels good the way a Band-Aid does. Secure.

I put my shirt back on and check myself out in the mirror. I think I look suspiciously lumpy. I go back to Janice 2's room. I put the nail scissors back and go through the suitcase on the luggage rack at the end of her bed. I take out a hoodie and bring it back to my room. It's pink and says "Juicy" in rhinestones, but it is good and bulky.

Marguerite doesn't say anything. "My options were limited," I say.

Today Bob went floor to floor knocking on doors, reminding us all about Mitchem's revival. "Salvation. Maple Room. Five p.m. Today and every day." Over and over. He handed out leaflets with the same information. Now the hallways are littered with them.

Marguerite has no interest. "Revival," she says, as if that says it all. And maybe it does. On the other hand (if I had another hand), the revival is something to do in between killing and eating. Undifferentiated time is the worst. There are no more three-day-long days.

I tell Marguerite about three-day-long days. The last one I remember was the summer before the last summer. We were having a dinner party and I had to get up early to mow the lawn before the bees were on the clover, and to fix one of the wooden folding chairs so we'd have enough for everyone. You cleaned and I cooked. And after everyone had left, even though it was so late, we watched an episode of "Madame Secretary" in which the Dalai Lama's death (pancreatic cancer) threatened to derail a climate accord between the US, China and India. But then the next reincarnation of His Holiness turned out not to be the American kid after all and everything worked out with some concessions to India on solar subsidies. That whole season was bad. Full of exposition masquerading as dialogue. But the last scene of that episode was moving. The monks destroying the sand mandala. Afterward, you kept me company outside while I had a cigarette. There was a nearly full moon that night. You said it looked pink and I said orange. You went up to bed and I washed a pan that had been forgotten outside by the grill. By the time I carried the cat up with me, you had turned out your light but had left mine on and had filled my water glass. I worked on a crossword puzzle until I couldn't keep my eyes open any longer.

There are no more three-day-long days. That feeling of abundance depended not upon excess and not scarcity, but finitude and a kind of thrift. It had to do with there being only so much time in the day but still more than just enough and using up every ounce of it, not wasting a moment. But to be undead is to be superfluous, perpetual. The moon is always full. We dream without sleeping. We refuse to return to the earth. Hunger is relentless.

The Maple Room is the larger of two conference spaces on the second floor. A dozen or so hotel guests stand around. A few sit against the walls. Several more lie on the dark green carpet like action figures pretending to sleep—flat on their backs, legs straight, arms at their sides, gazing at the high ceiling as if there is something fascinating up there. The walls are upholstered with mauve fabric and on one side there are tall windows with vertical blinds that don't close properly in some places so that bright slivers of early evening sunlight slice across the room.

Bob enters through an inconspicuous side door carrying Mitchem's side table. He sets it at the front of the room and stands aside. After exactly the right number of seconds, Mitchem strides in, hands held behind his back. He steps up onto the side table. He is wearing his usual clear rain poncho over highwater suit pants. He's got his damaged head wrapped in a white scarf that would look more like a bandage than a turban if not for the large, gold brooch pinned to its front.

"I am only able to share what I know." He begins talking so suddenly and so loudly it startles me. Even the hotel guests who have been lying down pay attention. "My meaning may not be clear. That does not matter. Nothing matters. My meaning. Your meaning. Meaning does not matter. Only hunger."

I feel roused and tired at the same time. I look around for Carlos or Marguerite.

"We all arrived here from the same place." He gestures

around at the walls, the windows. "We came here from life. A bleak and aimless world of uncertainty and self-delusion, of violence cloaked in compassion, of greed masquerading as order. A world of ranks and classes and races. Life. A world consumed by fear. A terrible world whose only consolations were the fantasies of god and of science. Life. We renounce that world. We renounce life. We turn our backs on its injustices. Its trivialities. Its delusions. We have made a new world! What do we call it, this new world?"

It is unclear at first that we are meant to answer this question. Bob is there to help. He steps up to the front and repeats, loudly, like the drill sergeant from a movie with a drill sergeant, "What do we call this new world?" Then he steps back again.

A skinny guy in a bicycle helmet who has been sitting cross legged not far from me stands up, "The world of the dead?"

Bob looks at Mitchem as if he is interested to find out if this is the right answer. Mitchem points at bicycle helmet man. "No!" his voice cracks into a disconcerting shriek. The man sits back down. Mitchem shakes his turbaned head as if he is astonished at this failure to comprehend. I for one am glad I didn't say anything.

"No," Mitchem says again, regaining his composure. "Not the world of the dead. The world of the dead is the world of worms and darkness." I notice for the first time how young Mitchem is …was …is. He is one of those men who must have looked forty when he was twenty. He continues. His voice rises. "The world of the dead is a place without hunger. Is that your world? Is your world a place without hunger?"

No one says anything.

Mitchem looks over at Bob. Bob shakes his head. Mitchem looks back at us. He looks suddenly tired in his poncho, like a folded up umbrella. "Do you live in a world of darkness?" He points to the windows. We all look. The blinds don't seem to hold the answer he's looking for. "No," he says. "You do not live in darkness."

A few tentative voices offer up weak agreement.

"Do you live without hunger?" There is some murmuring, some headshaking. "Do you? I'm really asking."

Someone near the back says no. Mitchem looks over at Bob.

Bob repeats the question for us. "Do you live without hunger?"

A few more hotel guests join in. Mitchem throws back his head and yells out the question at the ceiling. "Do you live without hunger?"

"No!" A few guests get to their feet.

"Then you do not live in the world of the dead!"

Someone shouts, "Fuck the dead!"

I slip out when more guests are coming in. I find Marguerite on the roof. She says she doesn't need a recap. Instead I tell her more about "Madam Secretary." Téa Leoni's husband on the show is also her husband in real life. On the show he is a religious scholar (and CIA spy handler). He would be able to explain the cult dynamics at work here. I muse about the writers' decision to include in a show about international politics a character able to opine on theology and philosophy. Of course it was not really a show about international politics, but rather a show about the relationship of idealism and pragmatism. The State Department was just the dramatic scaffold for a series of moral crises brought on by greed and machismo that were always resolved with a mix of earnest political compromise, economic strong-arming, late night leftovers and chance. Every episode it was the same. In that way, the show was more of a situation comedy. In that way, so was government.

—

Mitchem says that we have exceeded the previous confines of ontology. That our very existence has rewritten biological reality. That we have annihilated the ideas of both heaven and hell, which, he says, is the most striking and beneficial advance in human evolution to date. He says we are the apotheosis of humankind. He says we should envy neither the dead nor the living. He calls us the risen. He says we are the new divinity. He says, "Hunger freed from satiety is grace."

Mitchem holds up a coffee cup. It is a regular cup. "This cup," he says, "This cup can be whatever I say it is." He looks at it there in his own hand. I expect him to transform it with a magician's flourish into a bouquet of bright flowers. "This cup is the body. This cup is the soul." He pauses. I expect him to drop it. He looks at us. "Therefore …." He lets the silence hang there. "Therefore the body is the soul." We all look at the cup. I never trust it when someone says "therefore."

"But what about the cup?" I say to Marguerite later. I want to know what happens to cups in a world of metaphors. Is it more true that a cup is the body and the soul or that a cup is a cup? I know a cup when I see one, but I am no longer certain about the body and I never knew anything about the soul. So (therefore) maybe I shouldn't be so sure about cups.

Marguerite says, "None of this is real."

I say, "That sounds like something Mitchem would say."

She shrugs. "Some of it is real."

—

I am walking through the old Thriftway. Dreaming again. The store is flooded. Entirely submerged. I move down the aisles the way you move under water—more deliberately and with more surrender. The refrigerator cases glow eerily. I am worried the crow will come loose and float up out of reach.

The shelves are still stocked with jars of mustard and jam and cans of soup and cat food. Protein bars drift in suspension. Eggs have gotten out of their cartons. Large. Extra large. White. Brown. They bob gently along the floor. I nudge them with my feet, careful not to break them. They tumble unhurriedly.

An instrumental version of "The Sound of Silence" is playing. It warbles in the murk. I say out loud "Piped in," and it strikes me as clever. I sing along. It feels amazing. In the dream I wonder if it is because my lungs are filled with water. I am filled with water. I know all the words. But they are not right—not the actual words of the song. I think, I should make a music video for "The Sound of Silence!" I can't believe what a brilliant idea this is. I think I will make music videos for all the songs that came before music videos. It will be a sensation.

I want to see what the produce section looks like, but I am afraid the vegetables will be rotten and disgusting. I go to the freezer aisle instead. You are there. You have a bag of frozen peas in each hand. You are disappointed when you see me. You were going to surprise me with the peas, but now I've spoiled it. I try to start over and turn down the candy aisle instead, but it doesn't work.

—

My room phone rings. This has never happened before. My first thought is that I am dreaming, but I can tell by the quality of the sound that it is not part of a dream. It rings again and my second thought is that Bob must have figured out how to program the telephones. I sit up in bed. I look at the phone crouched there on the bedside table. When it rings, a red light flutters weakly inside the cube of clear plastic the way coffee sputters up into the top of a percolator pot. I imagine all the room phones ringing at exactly the same time all over the hotel, puzzled guests picking up.

"Hello?" we all say.

A computer says, "This is your courtesy wake-up call."

The message repeats and repeats. "This is your courtesy wake-up call."

Each time, just before the recording starts again, there is a hesitation in the flow of particles through space. A moment when I can hear the open line and I think it will be you there in that blankness. After I don't know how many times, the line goes dead. I sit on the edge of the bed with the phone to my ear. Now it is just a piece of plastic.

I hang up the phone. Count to five. Pick it up again. I dial 9 for an outside line. I get a dial tone. Before I can remember or forget our phone number, I dial it. There is a pause, then a tiny mechanical click, then the line pops open like a leak springing in the night sky.

Emptiness spills into me. My ear is the Panama Canal connecting two oceans of emptiness. The emptiness out there and an emptiness in me. Dark. Entire. Impossible. Emptiness teeming with cold silence. It is so silent it is loud. It is unbearable. It is so familiar.

I hang up.

I go into the bathroom, close the door, and turn on the lights. I climb up on the vanity and sit with my feet in the sink so I can get close to the mirror. I open my mouth as wide as I can. If I were alive, my breath would fog up the glass. I hold my jaw and tilt back my head to see past my teeth and tongue and down into my throat. I say "Ahhh."

Do you remember the time we were walking up Columbia Street and we saw something we thought was a backpack or a bulky sweater hanging in one of the gingkoes on Legion? It was dark and bunched up in the crotch of the tree. We were about a block away. As we got closer something seemed wrong with it. About it. Something seemed wrong about it. We were probably within twenty feet when we could tell it was alive. Maybe three yards and we somehow knew it was a swarm of bees even though neither of us had ever seen a swarm of bees. We knew it before we could see the bees themselves.

It was solid and liquid and crawling and black and shimmering. It was the body of one thing made out of the bodies of other things. One animal made out of other animals. It was a shimmering black octopus made of bees. Dripping bees. It kept reshaping itself into a new octopus. Bulbous head and webbed body and tentacles. It was horrifying and beautiful.

That's what is inside of me. Only instead of an octopus, it is hunger. Instead of bees, it is made of nothing. Hunger is an animal made of nothing.

Mitchem is standing on his side table. His eyes are closed. His voice sounds tired. He says, "Nothing can be more clear than the fact that nothing is real. Nothing is real. Nothing is real."

He keeps repeating this, "Nothing is real. Nothing is real," until I hear it differently. Nothing *is* real. Is he saying the opposite of what Marguerite says or are they saying the same thing?

He goes on saying it. "Nothing is real. Nothing is real." Until suddenly I realize he is talking about the swarm. I expect him to open his eyes and look right at me. I stand up. This whole time he has been talking about the swarm. He has looked inside and seen the same thing I saw. The same nothing. I can feel it shaping and reshaping itself inside of me.

Mitchem stops talking. There is a long silence in which it is possible to still hear him saying the same thing over and over. He opens his eyes but he doesn't look at me. He isn't looking at anyone. "Did you ever do something you never told anyone? Something shameful. Or something perfect." It sounds as if he is talking to himself, but his voice is raised. As if to be heard by himself, he must be heard by us. "It was probably not that bad, really, or that good. Something you did when you were a kid. And as you grew up, you knew it wasn't as bad or as good as you used to think, but maybe, you thought, maybe it *was* that bad. Maybe it was perfect. So you decided you would keep it in, to protect yourself. One way or another. You didn't tell your first girlfriend. You didn't tell a stranger in an airport bar. You decided, this is the one thing I will die with. I won't be alone because I will have this."

He closes his eyes again.

The sound of moaning. The sound of chattering teeth. The sound of the vertical blinds knocking against each other in the artificial breeze of the HVAC.

"I don't remember what it was," he says. He makes an exquisite pinching gesture in the air near his wrapped head then lets it go. "I've tried. I've tried. I've tried. I've tried. I've tried. But I can't feel it in there."

He opens his eyes. "It's gone. That one thing that only I knew about myself. That thing that made me me, alone in all the universe. I've lost it." He sounds filled with wonder.

He looks around at us. "This is what I want to tell you. It doesn't matter. It doesn't matter. Composed. Decomposed. We are unbound. We are hungry because we are endless. We are endless because it's too late. It's all over. It's all gone."

I leave the Maple Room. The clacking of teeth and the moans. I take the stairs instead of the elevator. It feels like escape. Two at a time. I am on the last flight to the basement before the second floor fire door finally swings closed on its slow hinges and the resolute sound of it shutting is like a bullet in my back. It knocks me down or knocks me out. My knees buckle. I reach for the handrail. I collapse on the steps. Who can say why every loss and deferred sorrow is consolidated in the door's incontrovertible latch, but for a minute I am undone. Untethered. I am the faint green glow of the exit sign over the door to the garage. I am cold concrete. I make a sound, a sob or a gasp, and I am that sound. Its echo condenses and settles like a vapor. I can feel it on my skin. The loss. The sick prickle of hunger. The swarm churns, reorganizes itself. I stagger to my feet.

This is what I do not tell you. I leave the hotel. I move through the streets like the zombie of a B movie — mindless-seeming, heeding an inaudible summons. The imperative of hunger.

I head north and east out of downtown, up through the grid of empty residential neighborhoods. Up narrow streets made narrower by encroaching weeds and blackberry vines. Rhododendrons and roses gone feral. Apple and fig trees heavy with fruit that will fall and rot. The fleshy citrus scent of magnolia blooms the size of baseball gloves. I startle a family of deer bedded down in an overgrown park. Playground fort. Swing set. I pass under the freeway and through an abandoned siege wall made of burned-out school buses. Through a strip of discount shoe stores and nail salons and pho shops. Through the empty reek of big box outlets about to lift off with the flap and coo of roosting pigeons. Through the parking lot wasteland.

This is the east. Higher, flatter ground that once was prairie, then farmland, then was cut and zoned and paved, and for a long time had been headed toward this future. Maybe the future of this future looks more like the past. Maybe the prairie will return.

It is nearing night by the time I come to the wide arterial boundary between one kind of sprawl and another. I am about to cross when not far away I see a pair of shadows dash across the road and disappear into a high laurel hedge on the other side. I clench my jaw to keep it from chattering. I can tell they are teenagers by how they move, or by how they hold hands as they run, or by the fact that they are stupid enough to be out here. I wait then I follow. I am cunning as a raccoon, inscrutable as a rat.

I emerge at the edge of a meadow that used to be a golf course. The pale blooms of Canadian thistle and Queen Anne's lace float ghost white in the dusk. Half a mile away on the other side of the fairway and beyond a solemn escarpment of trees silhouetted against the murky sky, the patchwork of prefabricated communities with cul-de-sacs and banks of locked mailboxes. Gated developments and ersatz estates surrounded by walls now crenellated with cinderblock battlements, festooned with barbed wire. Inside bonus rooms with boarded-up windows, the living are plotting their salvation. They are watching reruns. They are playing board games. They are updating the canned goods inventory, the history books, the Bible. They are teaching their children. They are sleeping. The living sleep. They give birth. They die. They sneak out to have sex on a golf course. Even now.

On the ground it is night now, but the sky still glows. I wade through a dark sea of long grasses. Fireflies blink on and off across the open field and up in the branches of trees. A fleet of tiny unheeded Paul Reveres uncovering their lanterns, covering them again, signaling danger, danger, danger.

I begin to see the intervals between their flashes as connective. A constellation of sentient stars separated by time instead of space. A viscous tick-tock in which I, too, am suspended. I feel it inside me. The static blankness of my arrested cells and the uncertain space between them. The gap between one blink of memory and another. The interval that is relationship. The body of the crow in the body of me. The black hole that is sucking me inside out, the utter unutterableness that I never entered when I was alive.

It is not what Mitchem says or what Marguerite says. Not nothing. Not real or unreal. It is not simple emptiness. Not lack. Not want. Not hunger. It is not hunger. It is grief.

I find I have stopped. I am in the fairway near a stand of pine trees at the edge of a water hazard grown in with cattails. The absence of the old, loud world is intense. Silence is a painful pressure. A blister. Small sounds brush against me, but do not give relief. Crickets, frogs, a killdeer. The cattails *snick snick* against each other. I say out loud, "It feels real." I think I am talking to myself. Or to Mitchem. Or Marguerite. Or maybe I am always only talking to you. But the crow answers. It says, "Apple. Arm. Ink. Crown."

Apple

Arm

Ink

Crown

The crow's words hang in the dark. Like the fireflies. Not like the fireflies. They are separate and not sequential. Simultaneous but not overlapping. They are periodic and persistent. The syntax is spatial, as if each word is pinned to a different wall of a room that is my body. I can only look at one wall, one word, at a time. Except there are no walls, just the night and my body and the words.

Apple

Arm

Ink

Crown

All around me there is an explosion of noise and motion, a rattling whoosh and a short, high shriek. The firefly delirium pops and I drop flat to my stomach. The grass thrashes wildly in a gale that blasts straight down from the sky. A heavy rain sweeps across my back. It takes two, three seconds before I understand the golf course sprinkler system is still working. I laugh out loud and clap my hand over my mouth.

Golf course. Sprinkler system. Zombies. Talking crows. Sometimes I think the world is better now.

I can't hear anything but the chat-chat-chat-rattle of the sprinklers and I can't see anything, but it doesn't matter. I know the living are nearby, but it doesn't matter. The hunger is there, but even that doesn't matter because I am floating on the late summer smell of grass. I am six years old and my father is holding my wrists in his hands and is spinning, spinning, swinging me in a circle. He is the center. My body flies out from him. I am a flag, a ribbon, a blur of light. My hair flies out. My feet fly out. My wrists sting in his grip. My arms will pull out of their sockets. I will arc out across the lawn and the uncut field and farther and farther from the roofed box of our house, higher and higher above it all, trees and roads growing smaller and smaller below, and near the apex of my arc I will exit the atmosphere into cold silent orbit. But he slows and I float down. My knees bump the lawn and are stained green. I try to stand and the earth tilts. I reel sideways like a drunk and fall. The grass is cool. I can't stop laughing. I can't stop crying. I am lying on my back in the long grass of the old golf course crying, except I can't cry. It is unbearable. Hunger lurches up, furious.

I feel for my knife and twist up into a crouch. The sprinklers rattle and hiss. Close by the two figures emerge from the dark grass. They dodge and leap around the sprinklers and disappear behind the tall screen of the cattails. They swear and laugh then hush each other. *Shit ouch shit shh shh quiet.*

I crouch crawl until I can see them at the edge of the pines. They stand in each other's arms, already naked and so alive. They glow in the dark like the white flowers, like allegorical statues in a midnight garden. Youth. Love. Stupidity. Lust.

Hunger surges through me. I move cat fast and launch at their legs.

After this, things are neither fast nor slow. Each thing is its own thing, related but not connected to the others. Like the fireflies. Like the words. Crawling up the tangle of their legs. Stabbing in the knife, deep and upward. The shrieking grunt. The pine needle duff. The fever chill that blooms in my chest like the smell of blood in the night air.

The crow is loud as one hundred crows shouting from a tree inside of me. I cannot tell what it is saying. Now or No or Know or You.

Everything is still. I lie still at the center of the hunger that is actually grief, my hand still on the knife still in the dead girl still on top of her still lover who is still alive and still unconscious or paralyzed by fear. Everything is still. The living, the dead and the undead. I press my cheek to the girl's naked back like it's the cool tile of a bathroom floor. Like it will soothe. But her skin is slick with blood and I turn my face and lick. You always said I was inconsolable.

Mitchem is wrong. We are just like the living. Hunger is only ravenous hope. A mirage. Always receding. The black swarm behind my teeth. There is no bottom to this well. No dark place to wait it out. Nothing will ever touch this craving for you. How long before we let ourselves know what we know?

—

I roll onto my back and lie on the soft duff with my arms spread. No. Just the one arm. Fireflies blink on and off in the branches overhead. I hear the boy struggling under the body of the dead girl. He breathes in sobs. He gets to his feet. I close my eyes. He wavers naked and luminous in my mind. He is not Love now or Beauty or Innocence or any other idea. He is only a boy. Only a boy now. I want to kill him. I keep my eyes closed. Maybe he will smash my head in with a rock. I keep my eyes closed. Maybe he has a gun. I keep my eyes closed. I become aware again of the sprinklers. Their methodical, manic chatter like the clacking of teeth. I keep my eyes closed.

Maybe a long time passes or maybe not much. I open my eyes. I am alone with the body. I turn her onto her back and run my hand over her blood-sticky skin to find her belly button. She is doughy and not well muscled. I imagine this had been her idea, to meet outside in the dark. I imagine she had to be convinced. I imagine it was their first time. I imagine it was routine. I see that life has gone on as always. I stab in the knife and pull it sharply up until I hit the hard intersection of her ribs. I think of trout fishing with my stepfather. The girl's insides coil and pool. The crow's dead flesh prickles against my undead flesh with the fizz of hydrogen peroxide in a dirty cut. I kneel there in the dark. I do not pray. I do not plunge my face into the trough of the girl's open carcass. I will never eat again.

I take off the ridiculous pink sweatshirt and draw the hood cords tight shut to make a sack. I cut loose her liver and kidneys and put them in. I carve off the soft belly meat, the easy cuts from her thighs, her calves. I take what I can carry. I do not know why I do this except I can't let go. I bundle closed the sweatshirt and sling it by its sleeves across my bound chest. I wipe my knife clean in the grass then think twice and plunge it into the ground. I stand and look out across the golf course. Same darkness. Same moon. The sprinklers chatter. The fireflies signal signal.

I go to the hotel. It is quiet. I go to my room. I stand in my bathtub. I take off my clothes, but keep on my bindings. They are stained red by the girl's blood. I make believe it is my blood. That I have been injured. That I can be injured.

I turn on the shower. The water runs rusty then clears. I stand in the stream for a long time. I think, *I want to cut off my hair.*

I leave my clothes and the sweatshirt full of dead girl in the bathtub. Bloody runoff pools around the drain.

The hallways are empty. The carpet absorbs the sound of my footsteps. I go to Janice 2's room for a change of clothes. I put on a summer dress with blue flowers. Bachelor buttons. I get the nail scissors from the back of the toilet. I take the stairs to the roof. Marguerite is there. She has been using an ax to break up furniture. Bedside tables, dresser drawers, chairs from the dining room on the first floor. The wreckage is piled up in the center of the open area. I help her gather up the last of the splintered remains, then we sit on the edge of the roof looking south at the moon. I think of the moon I saw last week. Or yesterday.

I say, "Why is the moon always full?"

Marguerite says, "What is it filled with?"

"Hunger?" I say.

"Grief," she says.

I want to hold the crow in my arms.

I say, "I'm not going to eat anymore. What I mean is that I will no longer eat."

Marguerite says, "I'm going to leave."

"Where will you go?" I say.

"Home," she says.

"Where is home?"

"Home is like the moon," she says.

"Filled with grief?"

"Never where you expect it."

I say, "Will you cut off my hair for me?"

I sit with my head between my knees and Marguerite snip snips close to my scalp. I imagine the curved blades of the tiny scissors are the teeth of a cat grooming me. Bite, bite, bite all over my head until I have only fur left. I can imagine going further. Asking her to cut off my ears, my nose, the fingers of my one hand, the hand itself. Lighter and lighter.

Afterwards I lie with my head in her lap. I say, "We tried to have a baby." She runs her fingers lightly over my new fur as if I am made of clean, dry sand. "I had a miscarriage," I say.

She says, "Cats can reabsorb their kittens."

I say, "I think our hunger is what we have instead of what we've lost."

She says, "None of this is real." I don't want her to stop petting my head, so I stay very still and don't say anything. "Some of it is real," she says.

—

Sometimes early in the morning I would get up and put on my coat over my pajamas and ride in the elevator down to the ground floor. This is when I was young and it felt exciting to live in a building with an elevator, so I never took the stairs. I would go out the side door of the building and down the alley to the park and walk under the street lamps. I had never lived in a place with alleys or streetlights. It smelled like ozone and chlorine and duckweed. Sometimes I would keep going west across the old bridge and up the hill as far as Division where I'd sit in the bus shelter and watch the skateboarders in the parking lot of the bowling alley. Their street lamp shadows would stretch and swing around the dark dial of empty parking spaces.

When they went off a curb or the raised part of the sidewalk outside of the Grocery Outlet, their wheels leaving the pavement so absolutely, it was as if they disappeared from radio contact. Blipped out into thin air.

Thin air.

Then it went one of two ways. The clatter or the catch. The board flipping out from under them and skidding on its back across the asphalt, or else the hard wheels latching back onto the ground. Everything coming undone or coming together in those few silent seconds between launch and landing.

In that fleeting moment I could hear everyone else asleep. I could hear the empty aisles of the grocery store and the bowling pins waiting at the ends of the lanes. I could hear the sky getting lighter in the east.

That's the voice of the crow.

The sudden silence of liftoff. The stars about to disappear. The moment before you know whether it is the end at last or just another continuation.

I say to the crow, "Say something."
The crow says, "Zipper. Toast. Glass."
It sounds like love.

I can tell I am dreaming because at first I am naked then the next minute I am wearing an emerald green nylon track suit. I'm in the girls' locker room. The air is heavy with steam, the surprisingly arrhythmic sound of showers, and the impossible fruit fragrance of every shampoo and conditioner you can imagine. All the surfaces are covered in yellow tiles. Not all the same yellow. Three different shades. I can't quite discern a pattern, but I can't believe there isn't one.

Marguerite comes in and sits down by me on the yellow metal bench. She has one towel wrapped around her body and another twisted up around her head. Her skin is moist and glowing. She leans over and says right into my ear, "Crows are highly intelligent." A locker slams in some other part of the dream.

"I know," I say. "There was a study with masks."

She keeps her voice low, her mouth close to my ear, and says the same words again with special emphasis, like it's code for something else. "Crows are highly intelligent."

"Everyone knows this," I say.

Later Marguerite comes to my room. I say, "I had a dream about you."

She says, "None of this is real."

I didn't plan to, but I tell her about the crow. I say, "The crow talks."

She concedes. "Some of it is real."

"What are you doing on the roof with all the furniture?"

"Building a time machine."

"I think grief is a time machine."

"Did the crow tell you that?"

"In the dream you were telling me to listen to the crow."

"Crows are highly intelligent."

"Those were your exact words."

"And what did you say?"

"I don't remember."

I say to the crow, "Who are you? Are you the you to whom I am speaking?"

The crow says, "Dog. Rain. Kelp."

"Are you the baby?"

It says, "Feet. Fall. Black."

We called the baby Ovenbird. I can't remember why.

"Are you me?"

The crow says, "Open. Rock. Woolly."

I say to the crow, "What do you want?"

I say, not as a threat, but because I want to know, "Do you want me to take you back out and put you in the ground?"

It says nothing even after a long time.

A crowd of hotel guests is gathered on the roof. Marguerite's pile of broken furniture has been transformed into a pyre by the addition of a sturdy post, a stake, at its center. The air is heavy with the smell of lighter fluid. It smells like any summer weekend. It smells like impending disaster.

I am not sure if this is a dream. I check to see if I have one arm or two. The elevator dings and the doors slide open. Carlos and Marguerite step out onto the roof. The crowd parts to let them pass. We are uncertain of how to behave. Are we audience members? Will we be called on in some way? Should we avoid touching them? Should we push them? The terrible ambiguity of postmodern theater. Carlos follows Marguerite, a few steps behind. He carries a coil of stiff orange pot warp over one arm.

Marguerite pauses when she comes to Mitchem. They face one another. Witchy hair crown. Swami headwrap. An understanding hangs between them. Like a spider web. Or maybe it is a misunderstanding. Whichever, Marguerite lifts one hand and brushes it aside then she turns away from him and walks the rest of the way to the pyre. She circles the stake counterclockwise. Carlos follows behind. When they've gone all the way around, Marguerite stops and turns to face us. She seems to consider. I want her to look at me.

She bends down on one knee and I think she is going to pray, but instead she unties her shoes. She takes them off and also her socks. She tucks one sock inside of each shoe and places the shoes next to each other. She stands and pulls off her shirt over her head, quickly but careful to not mess up her hair. Where breasts had once been, there are two long, sloping cuts. Cuts not scars. Unhealed, unbleeding cuts sutured shut with stitches like the lashes of closed eyes. It flashes through me that the eyes will open and she will look at me from the flat face of her body. I will meet that stare or I will look away. I will drop to my knees. I will cease to exist.

Marguerite is no longer paying any attention to Mitchem or Carlos or to any of us. She turns her shirt right side out, folds it, and sets it atop her shoes. She takes off her green pants and folds them on top of her shirt, tucks her underwear in a pocket. It is as if she is undressing to go for a skinny dip. Her clothes in a neat pile on the shore.

I have never noticed before the inkblot symmetry between the span of collar bones to shoulders and the span of pelvis to hips. Maybe because of the breast eyes, I can see Marguerite's body in a way I have never seen a body before, even yours. The thin twists of grey pubic hair. Her hands hanging at the ends of her arms, loosely gripping the air. The way the wrinkled skin bags a little over the tops of her knee-caps. Looking at her body is like looking at your face asleep. So unguarded and fierce. I will not see you grow old.

She takes Carlos's arm then, and he helps her over the jumble of broken hotel furniture. He positions her back against the stake and hands her the end of the rope to hold as he wraps the length of the coil around her and around her from ankles to neck and tucks in the tail. I remember the feeling of her binding the crow into my chest. I put my hand there now.

Carlos climbs back down from the pyre and turns to face Marguerite. We all look at her. Her eyes are closed.

Mitchem claps his hands together. Once. Loudly. It makes me jump. "Bob," he says. He gestures to Bob to bring his side table.

Marguerite opens her eyes. "Stop," she says. And he does. "Stop," she says again, to the rest of us. She looks up. "Stop," she says to the sky. It is low and empty except for the moon. I remember the feeling of her cutting my hair. The feeling of her petting my shorn head. At last she looks at me. "Stop," she says.

Marguerite has cut off her breasts and has braided up her hair and has built her pyre. She looks to Carlos. "How can we bear more of what is already unbearable." Carlos takes a pack of cigarettes and a lighter from a pocket somewhere inside his jacket. He uses his lips to pull a cigarette from the pack. He flicks open the lighter and strikes the flint. Everything else is motionless. Maybe I imagine I can hear the crackling of the tobacco catching fire. He flips the lighter shut and pockets it. He smokes the cigarette a little bit. Then he holds it out toward Marguerite, but she's past that. He nods and takes one more long drag. Then he tosses the cigarette into the pyre. There is time for half a thought before the lighter fluid sparks. Then a burst of flames and the sound of a giant sail snapping full of wind and an explosion of hot air punches us back. Immediately Marguerite begins to howl. She howls and howls without needing to take in a breath. A long, endlessly long, high howl. Not to herself and not like a wolf howling to another wolf, but like a wolf howling to the moon. She howls like howling is singing.

Carlos in midair, flung off his feet by the explosion. Bob huddled on the ground. Mitchem, back turned, arms raised to shield himself, his clear poncho lit up red and orange. And all the rest. Frozen in time. I am the only moving thing except for the flames and Marguerite's howl and the black swarm surging up in her open mouth.

They say a total solar eclipse will alter you forever. That when day turns to night, even if you know why, it feels like the end of the world. That really it *is* the end of the world for about three minutes.

There was an eclipse the summer before the last summer. Astronomers called the narrow band of perfect celestial alignment "the path of totality." Millions of people packed up their kids and grandparents into minivans and RVs and drove to where they could experience it most fully.

We stayed home. From our yard where we watched through special cardboard glasses we bought online, the sun was 95% obscured, but they say it's that last 5% that makes the difference between astronomical event and transformative experience. It was beautiful, though, from where we stood.

Marguerite's body is the thin sliver of sun that stands between watching an eclipse and losing your place in the cosmos. That last 5%. When she burns away, that boundary is lost. The black swarm comes loose.

Then there is a sound that is the end of all sound. The first moment of true silence. And that true silence is also the first true darkness. It flashes out in a perfectly round hole that is surrounded by a ragged corona of the pyre's light. Ravenous, it swallows up anyone it can catch. Carlos. Mitchem. Lee. Bob. Alison. At least one of the Janices. It even swallows itself.

It lasts forever then it is over.

And I am running.

PART 3

If I tell you that the city toward which my journey tends is discontinuous in space and time, now scattered, now condensed, you must not believe the search for it can stop.

—Italo Calvino

THIS IS WHAT THE END of the world always looked like. Eight lanes of freeway empty and grey in the red light of the setting sun.

Exit 105. Exit 104. Exit 103.

I run through the night. I am alone now except for the crow and hunger. Unfed, the swarm shapes and reshapes inside of me. The world is big and empty, but inside of me is even bigger, even emptier. Hunger makes me vast and bottomless. I run and I run and I run. I eat the road. I devour it.

Exit 102. Exit 101. Exit 99.

—

I used to have a running dream. In it the ground pushed back at my feet. Pavement or pine-needled moss. I sprang forward. It wasn't effortless, but I could have gone on forever. I had it in me. In my legs. In my feet. In my arms. In my entire body. I had the resources of the undead. In my dreams, I realize now, I was undead.

Exit 95. Exit 88.

Where did this start? What is the beginning of something that is not a story? There is only the place I always return to in my mind.

I am asleep with you in the dunes. Not asleep, but not awake in the usual way. Not asleep in the usual way. Asleep but for only a few seconds at a time. Only long enough to have the feeling of waking again and again, but still with my eyes closed. Aware again, newly aware, and again, of the sound of the ocean.

My ankles are crossed and you are using my thigh as a pillow. I can feel the weight of your head right now. A gull passes between us and the sun. Its shadow crosses our bodies. I can feel that fleeting coldness right now. We hold things in our bodies.

Because we are so small together in the vast expanse, so small together in the lee of the dune, beneath the sky, within the sound of the ocean and the warmth of the sun, we are more together than we have ever been or ever will be again. This is the very best moment we will ever share. It is a better end than beginning.

It *was* the end. But we did not know it then. You do not know the end has happened until later. Or you do not admit it. Looking back, you can see it. And you realize that all the time after that was just an effort to keep going as if it weren't already over.

I was a zombie even then. Ravenous eater of a world that was already the last of its kind.

Exit 82. Exit 81. Exit 79.

Maybe, I say to myself or to the crow, maybe that end, the end you can only see after it is too late, maybe that end is what makes a beginning what it is. What else is a beginning but the end of something else?

The crow says nothing.

Exit 77. Exit 76.

Or maybe, I say to the crow or to myself, the beginning hasn't yet begun. Maybe that is where I am running to. Maybe there is a time between end and beginning that is like the time between beginning and end. A time that is to middle as beginning is to end. Maybe this is that time. Middle but without the hope of resolution.

I find I have stopped. I am standing in the road. The sky is light in the east. The moon is in the west. It is perfectly round. I am not really thinking anything. I am just looking at the moon. It is silver and flat and serious. A wind comes up to me in the empty morning like someone I've met before or seen before but don't know, and a feeling comes over me. It is sadness. Not a sadness, but sadness. All of it. The whole history of sadness. Everything in me is sad and everything around me is a part of it. The cracked pavement, the moon, the abandoned cars, the gravity that holds them to the road. It is total. I am taken, or taken down. I drop to my knees.

And then the feeling passes. Leaves me. I look for it. In the moon. In me. Nothing but a new sense of the same empty.

"Crow?" I say aloud. My voice is the last damp match.

The crow says, "Sharp. Safe. Fold." Its voice is the improbable strike, the flame, the fleeting sulfur proof of my continued existence.

I take the next exit. Slow curve and slope. This is how it feels to surrender.

Exit 74. West because west is the direction of leaving behind. West because west is the last resort. I go west because west is where I remember you.

—

Truck stop. Minimart. Starbucks. Roundabouts. Missing person flyers tacked to telephone poles: Michael, Eric, Sandra, George. The road narrows from four lanes to three then down to two. A row of storage units with orange roll-up doors, still locked. A power substation. On the side of the road, side by side, a La-Z-Boy and an identical child-sized La-Z-Boy. Later, a nice desk. A fire station. School buildings: Home of the Falcons, Home of the Timber Wolves, Home of the Raiders. A church with an American flag in its belfry instead of stained glass. A taco truck. A tow truck on its side. A sign for the landfill. A lake with ducks. Periodically a drive-through espresso place.

Everything I encounter has the quality of having been encountered before. An always already feeling. And at the same time, everything I encounter is strange to me.

Have I been here with you? Did we come this way?

What is familiar because I have seen it before and what is just part of a familiar story? What is remembered and what is received? What is strange because I have forgotten it, or because it is new, or because this time I am on foot, or because this time I am undead, or because this time I am without you?

"Which parts are real?" I ask the crow.

"Shine. Mud. Slow," it says.

I come to a town that has the look of a picked-over yard sale. Furniture pulled out onto lawns that are small meadows, into crumbling driveways, into the street. Bedframes and mattresses. Dressers with their drawers tossed around. Sofas and easy chairs with sodden, sunken cushions. Coffee tables with buckled veneer. Kitchen tables. Kitchen chairs. A rocking chair. A bathroom scale. An exercise bike. An ironing board. A severely beaten filing cabinet lying on its side like the meaty body of a mob informant.

Wasp nests hunch up in the eaves. Blackberries, clematis and morning glories hide the front porches, vining high up into the trees and over powerlines that sag with dangling pairs of shoes. Shoes pulled from feet, I think.

Someone before leaving this place lined up all the garden gnomes on the side of the road. They stretch from one end of town to the other, ready for a parade. They smoke pipes and hold shovels and sniff yellow flowers. One squints through the sights of a double-barreled shotgun. One sits on a toilet reading a magazine. One holds a sign that says "Welcome." Another holds a sign that says "Go to Hell."

The next town is the same and different from the last. The houses are all nearly identical. All small and all painted white with blue or grey or green trim, or green or blue-grey with white trim. All claimed by vines. But nothing that belongs inside is instead outside. And all the gnomes are still in their own yards, hiding in the long grass of lawns that haven't been mown since forever. And the trees are different in this town. Here they have a loved look. The emptiness is less eerie and more sad.

I go from house to unguarded house.

From room to silent room.

In beds and in bathtubs, in easy chairs and in cars parked in dark garages, I find the townspeople. Long dead. Sunken and dry in their clothes. Some in suits and nice dresses. One in a football uniform, complete with helmet. The old and the middle-aged and the young and the too young. Couples in each other's arms. Whole families together. Even the family pets.

Razors. Pills. Guns. Gas. Little vignettes. Dioramas of the departed and their remains. I am the only ticket-holder at a suicide theme park. I look at their framed photographs. At their keepsakes. At their embroidered pillows. I tilt my head a little to read the spines of their books. I sit down at their kitchen tables. I study their refrigerator doors—school lunch menus, yearbook portraits, prom photos, a jury duty summons. I look out of their windows. I stand in the slow sparkling swirl of their dust and feel them shiver. I am what they feared so much.

Eventually there are only barns folding in on themselves and remnant reaches of white board fence dividing up feral farmland, cows and deer and horses grazing together in the long grass. I'll bet it didn't take long for coyotes to take out all the sheep and alpacas. The line of a river to the south is a greener, thicker ribbon of willow and alder.

The roadbed is built flood-high above the valley floor. Scotch broom and blackberries scramble up its steep gravel shoulders. The asphalt is grey and frost-heaved and crumbling into weeds. There are mile markers. Speed signs spangled with bullet holes.

No vehicle has gone this way in a long time, but there is something left in the pavement, in the engineered curves, the way there is something left in me. It still vibrates with panic. We hold things in our bodies. The earth holds things in its body. In clay. In ice. The real. The unreal. Time. Each other. All the chances we had.

—

The madness of hunger or the madness of grief or just plain madness.

Would I eat a baby? If there were a baby lying in the road, would I eat it? Yes. I would eat a baby. Would I eat you?

Fasting makes sense of the hunger. The constant internal grasping. The only sensible answer to this is to always withdraw the thing after which I grasp. To subvert. To thwart. To deny. It closes the loop. If I am hungry and I eat and I remain hungry, hunger becomes rage. But to deny fulfillment makes sense of the hunger—I don't eat, so I am hungry.

The hunger crouches. It sulks. It blames. And I ignore it. Or I do not ignore it. I say, Yes, I know. And still my answer is no. I am parenting my hunger.
    I say to the crow, "You can't be a friend to your hunger."
    The crow says, "Robin. Jump. Sweet. Hum."
    I know that it is right. "I'm not ready," I say.
    "Tooth. Smoke. Switch."

During the day, the wind blows. I walk into it and walk into it. I think if I open my mouth I will fill like a windsock. It drops again when dark comes. I stand in the road and watch the sun set behind the western hills. I remember singing and reverence.

I meet no one living or dead.

PART 4

She lost the veined blue book of her thoughts.

—Dionne Brand

A HOUSE STANDS BY ITSELF on the far side of a field that rolls up to the edge of the forest. I leave the road, take the long cut of a rutted drive across acres of hay still green at the stems. Toppled by its own weight, it lies in great whorls and waves. Swallows reel and tilt. Grasshoppers stridulate. Yes, stridulate. You would say, how do you know these things? I would shrug and say, how does someone know anything?

I am close before I see the house has been gutted by fire. Its white clapboard facade stands like a theatre flat painted to look like the front of a house. Through the empty window frames, a roofless blackened hollow. "Like me," I say to the crow.

Behind the house, I find another smaller house untouched by the blaze. The place you keep someone you are obligated to keep—a mother-in-law. Or someone who is obligated to keep you—a caretaker. I go in.

The moldering leaves of morning glory vines paper its windows brown. Tobacco stained light. A gardening magazine folded open to an article on tomatoes. Yellowed newspapers in a stack by the woodstove. A glass on the bedside table. A shower curtain that is a map of the world. Salt- and pepper-shaker birds. A cracked cake of green soap. A wall phone the same color. Its long cord is stretched and hockled.

I lift the receiver and put it to my ear. "Hello?" Only the ordinary nothing.

I lie down on the bed. I sit at the kitchen table. I sort through the contents of a mason jar. Rubber bands, used twist ties, pen caps, a purple packet of powder for extending the life of a grocery store bouquet, lengths of twine bundled into tidy little hanks, some keys on rings, others loose, cup hooks, picture hooks, picture nails, a pair of tweezers, two books of matches. I compile a picture of the old woman I will never be. I know everything about her. I line up the odds and ends on the kitchen table and one at a time drop them into the hole that is my mouth. Odds. Ends. Nothing ever reaches the bottom of this well. Silence.

I can see now that I have been trying to outrun the swarm. I can see it is futile.

I say to the crow, "I think we will stay." The crow has nothing to say, but I can feel it in there making up its mind.

I thought I would want to live in the little house, but I prefer the garden. You would say, If I were a faerie, this is where I would live.

There are two old trees. An apple and a plum. They reach to each other, are collapsing slowly into one another's arms. Branches as thick as trunks themselves. The plum is a mess of tender red-leaved watersprouts shooting up from old and new breaks. It is heavy with reddening fruit. The trunk of the apple is hollow like me as if it should be undead like me and yet it is not. Yellow apples weigh down the unpruned ends of the tree's few branches so they touch the ground.

It is clear there is no simple beginning or simple ending. Every live thing is the history and future of all dead things. Every dead thing is the future of all live things.

I lie down in the bower created by the plum and the apple. I look up through the branches to the sky. Small suns dapple my body. I feel the way I did the summer I moved into a tent in my mother's backyard and read all the Narnia books. The summer of the portable typewriter. The summer of peach paper and green ink. I feel something else is possible.

A bird—a dapper scrub jay—lands on my forehead and tilts its head so we are eye to eye, and in that meeting a clue is conveyed that reveals a mystery that wasn't a mystery until there was the clue. Not the kind of mystery that can be solved. Not a mystery of what happened or who did it or even why. This has all been known for so long. The kind of mystery that is a sacrament.

When the jay pushes off into air, it leaves on my skin the firm live impression of its departure.

I am lying on the ground between the two trees. I lie in the same position without moving. The crow is lying inside of me, just as motionless but more alert.

At first I only hear the birds and when they are not there I think it is quiet. But after a while—a long while, I think—I notice that I am having an idea instead of hearing. And when I notice the idea, I instantly stop having it. Like when you are not very deeply asleep and you become less deeply asleep because of a click in your brain and then you are suddenly aware you were more deeply asleep than you knew but also aware that even now you are not yet exactly awake.

Once I stop having the idea, I realize it is not quiet at all. Sometimes it is very loud. The leaves are loudest. They crackle and hiss and make a high sung sound. The dirt is loud, too. Always sighing. Not a tired sigh or a wistful sigh. Not resigned, but almost. If resignation could be resolute.

I feel as if I am holding on to something, to the edge of something or to the end of something. Everything is going so fast. The light coming very quickly and the dark, too. The planet spinning and me pressed here on its surface. Every moment is the moment I know I am not going to be able to hang on. About to slide off over and over. It takes all my willpower to not let go and at some point I decide it doesn't matter so I do let go. But I was not actually holding on to anything so the feeling does not go away. Then I have the feeling of needing to let go and the feeling of having let go at the same time.

This—*this*—is what it feels like to be undead. And this is what it felt like to be alive.

And then at some point it all slows down and there is only choose to move or choose to not move. It is like the hunger.

Do I move now? Do I move now? Do I move now?

—

I remember a room that had curtains with cherries and birds. Wind came in the open window and lifted them up from the sill and something made a *tick tick* sound. Somewhere in the house a door slammed. I was already awake, but then I was more awake. I did not move right away. The bed was still made and you were not there. I had fallen asleep with my clothes on. My arms and legs felt syrupy and useless. I heard the rain coming across the cut grass and then on the porch roof and I knew if I did not get up and close the window it would pool on the windowsill and wick up into the curtains, which already were stained with the tea brown tidelines of previous storms. I felt great regret. The regret of having to get up to close the window was just the loose end of all the other regret in my entire life. I sat up on the edge of the bed. I crossed the room. I closed the window. The sash weights knocked in their chambers.

Do I move now? Do I move now?

It was winter and we'd been sent outside. The snow was deep and fresh and still coming down. There was no color. The trees that were near looked black. The trees that were far away looked like the breast feathers of an etched bird. The sky was white. The falling snow looked grey as cinders. I lay in the snow, in the impression of my own body. I felt the snow leaching away my warmth. I closed my eyes. Listened to the tiny jagged collision of each flake falling into the others that had fallen before it. Millions on millions. White noise. It surged into my ears.

Do I move now?
Do I move now?

I think of all the time I spent deciding. Imagine what I missed. My whole life. I know again that I missed it all with you. Almost all of it. It's always so bad when I realize this again. But it is also always when I love you most. The sick kick in my stomach and the time-lapse bloom of something like my heart go together now.

Lying in the dunes with you. Sound of the ocean. Sound of wind in the dune grass. The same sound. No difference between ocean and wind and you.

I discover I don't have to decide to move or to not move. I can lie here for a hundred years. Five hundred. The squirrels sit in the branches and eat the plums, dropping the red skins and pits onto me. The apples fall heavily and make a vinegar smell. All the leaves fall. I am covered in leaves. The rain falls.

At first it is a relief to have stopped deciding, and then it's not. It is not a relief and it is not hard. To not decide. To not move. I thought it was hard, but then I realize it isn't actually.

At some point I find I am getting up without having decided. I wish I could lie back down and cover myself again with the leaves, but it is too late.

I leave the garden behind the house behind the house. The apple tree and plum tree are bare as the old women we will not be together. They hold each other.

—

It is winter now. I continue west.

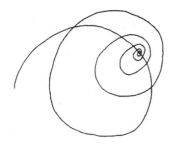

PART 5

It's so quiet in the world. One can hear the old river, which in its confusion sometimes forgets and flows backwards.

—Charles Simic

I COME TO AN INTERSECTION of two roads. Four stop signs stand facing out. Cardinal markers: stop, stop, stop, stop. It makes me think of Marguerite.

I recognize the bare sky and that sense of having farther to go than we realized. We'll come to the poplar plantation soon. Things in rows and ranks are mournful. Trees planted to pulp. Soldiers or their gravestones. Multiplicity and order reveal sameness and variation. The limitations of our individuality. That we can be felled.

"I know where we are," I say to the crow.

The crow says, "Cat. Brick. Water."

"We'll see the poplars soon." I say. "Or maybe we won't."

Unlike every other loss that took us by surprise, we always expected the trees to have been harvested. Every time, it was only after we had already resigned ourselves to the heartbreak that we realized it was just that we hadn't gone far enough.

And then there they still are, miles away yet. Even from here there is a sense of order that sets the plantation apart from the rest of this landscape. It has more affinity with the long, straight furrow of the raised road than with other trees. The bare-branched grey of the regimented thicket catches the lowering sun like a layer of upslope fog hovering between the sodden gold of unmown fields and the dark crest of fir-covered hills.

The last smudge of sunset fades before we reach the trees. I sit down in the road to wait out the rest of the night. I lie back and look at the moon and stars until they are smudged out by a fog that condenses close to the ground. It is cold and prickles my cold skin. It attenuates and disperses the small noises made by things moving in the untended fields to the south of the road and the plantation to the north. The shuffle of leaf litter. The snap of small branches. An owl nearby and another answering far away.

I ask the crow what it thinks.

It says, "Bitter. Rock. Bog."

I think about it. "Maybe," I say.

I dream that I am reading a book about the Donner Party. In it there is a long list, an inventory, of all the things they left along their way across the continent—furniture, mirrors, broken wheels, dead children, cutlery. I think, This is a poem. I fold the book closed in my lap, marking my place with my finger, and imagine a chapter that isn't there, about how they became lighter and lighter and lighter. I write a description in my dream mind of the matriarch Tamsen Donner, whose name I somehow know. It is the most perfect description ever written. In the dream, I close my eyes and repeat the words to myself again and again, telling myself not to forget.

—

It is gone by the time I hear the sound of footsteps approaching from the west. The sun is up somewhere, the fog is thick and the world is blank. The road is like my dream, disappearing in either direction.

I get to my feet and straighten the cornflower dress.

A figure emerges from the fog. It is Carlos. I think of the little green truck. I can feel its little wheels driving up my arm.

He is wearing an old fashioned baseball uniform. White knickers and a white jersey tucked in and belted. "Pirates" is written in swishy red script across his chest.

"Carlos," I say.

"Call me Pirate 26," he says, and turns slightly to show me the red number on his sleeve.

"Okay," I say.

"Come with me," he says.

He turns and I follow. The number 26 is printed larger on his back. I look at it as we walk and think, I know this number. It feels like the crow.

There is a turnoff and a plank bridge that goes over a culvert and across the irrigation ditch to the poplars. They are parted by a straight dirt road that vanishes in the fog before its vanishing point. There is a barbed wire fence and a chain-link gate, where Pirate 2 is waiting to swing open the gate for us and close it again after we pass.

Inside the fence, to either side of the drive, several more Pirates wait like gothic saints at the entrance to a cathedral, each sentry standing in one of the hundreds of shadowy vaults that open between the rows of trees, Pirate 37, Pirate

18, Pirate 4. Maybe eight all together. Some go ahead of us and some fall in behind.

I want to ask Carlos what is happening, what happened, how he got here. But the trees say *sshhh* and I say nothing. Their trunks are straight and branchless for twenty feet or more. Their limbs meet high overhead like the clasped hands of children playing London Bridge, a game I had forgotten until this moment but which comes back now along with the thrill and startle and slight sickness of being the one captured and held prisoner. *Take the key and lock her up. Lock her up. Lock her up.*

We walk into the trees for a very long time. Longer, I think, than is possible without reaching the limits of the rows. We keep going when it gets dark and are still walking when it is light again. The sameness makes it seem we are not making any progress at all. The trees just repeating and repeating. I feel confident but no longer care that something is different about how time and space are operating here. We walk and walk and the fog never fully lifts, though sometimes it thins and I can see deeper into the woods. Every step, every slight change in position, reveals a new pattern of tree trunks and pathways radiating outward.

The crow says, "Egg. Biscuit. Hat."

I don't answer.

It may have been several days by the time we arrive at a large, irregular clearing surrounded on all sides by more poplars.

There are Pirates occupied in various cooperative pursuits. Some glance up as we arrive then return to their tasks with little or no acknowledgment. A nod. A wave. Two Pirates sit at a card table working on a jigsaw puzzle. On the far side of the clearing there is a group doing tai chi. One group is moving a prefab shed that looks like a miniature red barn. They have it resting on peeled poles that serve as rollers. Two Pirates shoulder thick ropes attached to massive eye-bolts in its front corners, three push from behind, and two more move each pole from last to first position in turn as the shed creeps steadily forward. They work efficiently, trading clipped teamster-like calls. "Hup!" "Whoa-up!" "Steady!"

The other members of our entourage peel away in ones and twos to join various activities. Eventually Carlos and I are on our own. We pass a group that sits in an assortment of aluminum and plastic lawn chairs drawn into a loose circle. It looks like a twelve-step meeting. None of them are talking as we pass by. Maybe they are meditating. One of them looks just like Janice 3, and I whisper to Carlos, "Is that Janice 3?"

He says, "That's Pirate 12."

I look around at the other Pirates to see if I know anyone else. It is hard to tell with the fog and the uniforms — everyone looks both identical and familiar, but then I see Bob go by pushing a legless Pirate in a wheelbarrow. Bob is wearing the number 99. I say to Carlos, trying to start a conversation that leads somewhere, "99 seems like a good number." He shrugs.

"We drew them from a hat," he says.

"What if you don't like the number you get?"

"Any number can become lucky."

"Where's the hat?" I ask.

"In there," he says, indicating a corrugated metal structure on the far side of the clearing.

"Why the uniforms?"

"They were here."

"Do I get one?"

He shrugs.

"You used to be more forthcoming," I say.

He leads me to an octagonal gazebo set up roughly in the center of the clearing. It has a flimsy metal frame with screen panel walls and a cheerful yellow-and-white striped vinyl roof. Two Pirates are stationed outside. One I don't know, but the other is Alison. She is wearing the number 7, so I say, "Hi, Pirate 7."

She says, "*Your life ain't built on nothing*," and steps aside. The door of the gazebo is just one of its walls with hinges and a knob that is more like a latch.

"I'm supposed to go in?" I say.

She says, "*Birds fly to the stars, I guess.*"

I look at Carlos.

He shrugs.

I shrug back.

I open the door, step in, and close it behind me.

The gazebo is empty. In the center of the floor, which is just bare ground, there is a hole about ten inches in diameter. It looks perfectly unnatural. The edge of the hole does not crumble inward, but neither does it appear to be reinforced in any way...it is not the end of a pipe, or the top of a well. A stubble of orchard grass grows right up to the hole's edge and then stops absolutely. Not like the maintained edge of a lawn or the eroded edge of a cliff or even the edge of a terrarium. More like the edge of the universe. Utter and confounding.

It seems that something must either come out of the hole or go in. I look around for something to toss in. I walk all the way around the hole. I don't even find a rock large enough to be called a pebble.

I step near to the hole and peer in. The darkness in the

hole is not the darkness that it should be. It is some other darkness. Too profound.

I take off my right shoe. It is dirty and wet and the top has split from the sole along the outside. The gum tread is worn smooth and there is a hole in the heel the size of a silver dollar.

I drop the shoe into the hole and listen. It isn't just that I don't hear it reach the bottom. It makes no sound at all.

Goodbye sneaker.

It seems right to send the other one after it, so I take off my left shoe and drop it in, too. It is a relief. It's less a choice than a recognition or an admission.

I take off the cornflower dress. It has the look of something blown off a clothesline and found in the spring after the snow has melted. I drop it in.

I unwind my bed sheet bindings and drop them in one length at a time.

Then it is just the crow and me. I reach up under my ribs and take it out. Little red mummy. I unwrap it and toss the shirt sleeve in the hole. I hold the crow in my hand. Do I have to let you go? Even you?

It doesn't say anything.

It is folded tight in its own wings. It is light and dry. Its feathers are disheveled and beautiful. The little pads of its curled feet are still tender.

I drop it in the hole.

I picture it hurtling through an old pneumatic tube system and launching into clear sky.

I picture it opening like a parachute.

I picture it flying away.

I become aware that I feel heavy. My whole mud body feels like something I've been carrying. The feeling is very faintly familiar. I just can't stand up any longer, not even to back away to a more comfortable distance from the unnerving hole. I sit down next to it. That is good, but lying down would be better. I stretch out on the ground.

Naked. One-armed. Crowless.

We are picking blueberries. We have driven out to the coast to pick blueberries and have gone deep into the untended rows. We cannot see each other among the tall bushes, but we are close. The berries make a soft, solid sound as we drop them in the pails we have slung across our chests on baling twine bandoliers. Like the sound of fingertips tapping on each other. We lapse in and out of silence. The rest of the day is far away. Mourning doves call to each other from some other place. Blackberry vines muscle their way in. Deer have slept here.

It is late for picking in a summer as hot as this has been and many of the berries have dropped and are withering in the musty leaf mulch. I picture a bear snuffling them up and I say, "I hope we don't meet a bear." You say, "I hope we don't!" And I say, "It wouldn't be a bad way to die." I ask you how you would like to die. You have an answer ready. You say, "In my sleep after a good day."

I look up at the sky. The sun is bright and dull as a lightbulb behind clouds that move so fast I lose my balance. The crow flies over. It is glossy and full of wind. Its wings make a taffeta sound. It tilts its head and we look each other in the eye. It says, "Cake. Mountain. Forever."

I close my eyes and try to breathe but the end of the world is in my throat. The summer before the last summer. You are saying something about your brother or mine. I can hear you clearly but it is also as if you are far away. It is unbearable to look back from the future we did not know we had been traveling toward. That is not right. It is unbearable because we did know. It was plain as our own palms.

We move through the bushes picking as we go, pausing when one of us comes to a good bush. We have to reach deep in and bend down the highest branches to get the berries. Sometimes they slip loose from our fingers and drop to the ground. It feels like a waste. It feels like a tithe. It feels like how this place will be without us.

We go so far we come to the end of the rows where the grass is long and thick at the edge of the first cranberry bogs and the sun is warm and the sound of the ocean a mile away expands to fill the open space. All we can do is stand with our faces turned to receive the vaulted roar.

We walk back to the shingled shack where there are no windows in the window frames and no door in the door-frame and never anyone but us. We empty our pails into cardboard flats that are piled in the corner for this purpose and weigh our berries on the rusty white scale. Our footsteps are dull and dark on the worn floorboards. We realize we forgot to bring the checkbook but I find a twenty dollar bill in my pocket, which is a dollar more than we need and feels like cosmic ratification of our happiness.

We get in the car and drive to the beach. Our fingers are blueberry stained.

We go you-then-me through the beach pines and out into the dune grass. Whatever sound our footsteps make is swallowed up by surf we can't see until the last rise when all the shining world comes into view and we are like two piles of leaves picked up by the wind. Everything that was separated into you and me is thrown together and tossed up into the sky.

We leave our shoes and socks at the edge of the world and

cross the long slope to the spill of waves. From far away the wet sand looks just like the sky but up close it is like brown feathers or scales.

This is not the day we fall asleep in the dunes. This is the day there are ravens. Their heads are big as draft horses. They play some game we don't understand but like to watch. It is the day we almost don't notice thousands of birds migrating south, their endless, fearless flight, the perilous dotted line they thread down into the troughs and along the breaking crests. You give me a quartz stone you pick up at the edge of the water. Smooth and flat for worrying. We remember another day we found so many sand dollars we couldn't fit them all in our pockets.

In the car on the long drive home, I say, "I'm falling asleep." And you say, "Sleep, baby."

I hear the crow. "Shovel. Bone. Chair. Needle."

I wish that I had opened my eyes. I wish that I had turned from the window and looked at you in that moment when you were looking at me. This world slipped by me.

It is night in the gazebo. I am going to be sick. I sit up and heave over the hole's terrible edge. The black swarm hurtles out of me. It pours over my tongue and out of my nose. It comes in waves. I think there can't be more and there is. It seems like one continuous thing, an endless liquid body coming out of my body. I realize it will never end. I will always be vomiting. It will turn me inside out. I will vomit until I am gone. I don't know how long it goes on. When it is over, it is absolutely over. But it's hard to believe. I lie back. I wait for it to start again. But it doesn't.

After a while I can hear again. The specific noises of quiet. I look for the hunger, but there is only absence. I feel for the crow and find its empty space. I am at last bereft.

I pretended everything would be okay because it seemed impossible to always be saying goodbye. To blueberries. To the ocean. To ravens. To pelicans and plovers. To the cormorants. To the sunlight on the living room wall at four o'clock. To the sound of you in the next room.

I sit up again. I can see clearly. It is as if the darkness is lit by a darker darkness radiating from the hole or from me. All the shadows have shadows. Marguerite is there. Pirate 14. I realize that I knew I would see her again.

"It wasn't the right day," I say. "It wasn't the day in the dunes."

"Right day, wrong day," she says. "Put these on."

She sets a stack of neatly folded clothes on the ground next to me. Not a uniform. I pull on the white cotton underpants and undershirt. There are clean socks, too. The pants are a gabardine made of a nice lightweight wool. Marguerite helps me when I struggle to do the buttons of the shirt with just one hand. She pulls the empty shirt sleeve through the sleeve of the soft, green cardigan and tucks them together neatly into my waistband. I manage the belt on my own, but need help with the new white laces of the canvas sneakers. She ties them in double bows and then stands up. "Are you ready?" she asks.

It is very still in the clearing. Carlos is not there. Alison is gone. No one else is about. The fog has lifted and the moon is bright. Each stubbly blade of grass and each grain of dirt casts a perfectly crisp shadow.

We go into the poplars. They glow in the moonlight. There is a very thin, cold breeze. It rattles the few leaves that still cling high in the branches. We walk through the night. The wind drops and then lifts again just before sunrise.

The trees sway in and out of time, scissoring the morning light into flickering scraps and dapples. Their orderly trunks coalesce and dissolve in patterns of points and lines to either side. Where the lower limbs have been pruned away, there are eye-shaped scars. They stare past us, mesmerized by the many vanishing points arrayed spoke-like from every intersection of the orthogonal grid.

I like walking in my new clothes. I like the green of my sweater. I like having the empty sleeve tucked into my waistband. I put my hand in my pants pocket and it is almost like having two arms again.

Here and there are strange reminders of a past before the past was everything before the end. Garbage hauled into the woods instead of the dump. By-kill caught in the plantation's net. A mound of green wine bottles and quart-sized cans. An old wood cookstove. A fiberglass rooster the size of a cow, watching watching from its faded flat eye, about to speak. I miss the crow.

We walk until we're walking out instead of walking in.

We come to the gate at the edge of the plantation.

"This is goodbye," Marguerite says. I wonder if we are going to hug. She reaches into the back pocket of her uniform knickers and takes out a white stone. It is the stone you gave me on the beach. She holds it up to my face and waits for me to open my mouth. She places it on my tongue like a communion wafer. It is both smooth and slightly porous, pleasing, a nice weight, a little salty.

She opens the gate for me to pass and closes it again behind me. I don't know what to say and I am afraid I'll accidentally let the stone drop down my throat. Into what, now? What is there without the swarm? Without the animal made of nothing. Without hunger.

Marguerite reaches over the gate and gives my shoulder a good flat pat like it's the flank of a horse she's sending me off on. "You'll be fine," she says. She puts her hands deep in her pockets and heads back into the plantation. She turns once and I give a wave she doesn't return.

PART 6

If the end escapes us where are we?
—Hélène Cixous

I CONTINUE WEST. I KNOW you will not be there in the dunes. Except that I will be there. I will be there and through me you will be there. I think, if I am in the place where we were together, then we are together again.

Folds of dark forest and doleful clearcuts. A line of transmission towers stilting past two by two, empty-handed except for a dark hank of cable that sways like the rope left after a lynching. On the ridges, rusted turbines moan in the wind.

Overhead there are vultures. Dry birds with sharp eyes. They tilt their bald heads to watch my passage. Hold their tongues.

The road winds up into the low hills that separate the long river valley from the coast. There are landslides and washouts. To one side the land rises, to the other, it falls away steeply.

Uphill is the history of timber. Stumps hunker in the thicket of regrowth like gravestones in an untended cemetery. Downhill is the river and a set of old railroad tracks.

The bent stalks of winter weeds bristle up between the ties. Just off the road is a structure. Barely a shack. Its walls are a patchwork of plywood and tarpaper. I am about to take a step toward it when I see there is someone coming from the west along the tracks. I hear their steps crunch on the rough gravel ballast.

It is a woman, I think. Something in the slope and weariness of bulk. She walks with a walking stick and her dark oil cloth duster is so long it brushes the ground. She wears a grubby canvas satchel across her chest. Her hat looks like a mushroom cap. She moves slowly, with the familiar pain and determination of an old person. She is alive. I wait for the dark stab of hunger, but there is nothing but emptiness.

She stops, listening, and I expect her to look up the hill to where I stand more still than a tree. The sound of the river is brittle and faint in the cold. She glances back the way she came, as if checking to make sure she has not been followed, then steps quickly off the tracks and goes to the shack. She knocks on the wall.

"You up, sleepyhead?" She tilts her head to listen for a response.

A child answers. "I'm hungry." Petulant, whining.

"I'd swear to god you have a hollow leg," says the old woman.

"I do not," whines the child and thumps the wall. "I'm hungry."

The old woman lifts the satchel over her head and takes from it a series of items, placing them on the ground with precision and care. A length of rubber tubing. A hand gun. A wooden spoon.

The child pounds and kicks the walls of the shelter.

"Hold your horses, mister," says the old woman. She takes off her duster and spreads it on the ground. She lowers herself to it, kneeling first then turning painfully to sit. She leans her back against the shed, legs out straight. She rolls up her left sleeve. The arm is missing up to just below the elbow. She unwraps the bandaged stub, working with the practiced efficiency of a field medic. She uses her teeth to hold the end of the rubber tubing and ties a tourniquet a few inches up from the stub. While she works, she talks. She tells the child about a fish she caught this morning. A rainbow trout. She describes cutting it open and finding a whole mouse inside its belly. She falters sometimes from the pain. The whole time the child kicks and scratches on the walls of the shelter.

The old woman puts the handle of the wooden spoon between her teeth and lies down on the ground on her jacket. She wriggles a little to get in position. She slides open a small door, like a makeshift pet door, and inserts her arm. She doesn't even have it in as far as the tourniquet before the kicking and thumping stop. Her face contorts in pain. Tears slide from her eyes.

It does not sound like what you think. There is no animal snarl. It is just the sound of eating.

She opens her eyes and is looking directly at me. In the moment it takes for her to register what I am, in the moment before I turn and run, something passes between us. A recognition. What is unbearable is already too much. How can there be more?

As the road drops down out of the hills, I come again to the river. The bridge is out. The stump of the bridge's far end reminds me of the stump of the woman's arm or mine, the stumps of the clearcuts. These stumps are not alike, but they are all in the family of stumps.

The river is low in its bed. There are gravel islands. It is crowded by willows and alders. In the leafless canopy I can see here and there a bird nest laid bare. Which am I—the abandoned nest or the tree that holds it?

Night comes. Everything is bigger and closer in the dark. The stars are very thick. I understand finally that the sky is not above me, but that I am in the sky. This is related to the crow. And the crow is related to the baby. And the crow is related to you. Maybe the way the baby was related to you. Not through blood, but through me. Through a particular shared longing for increase. We wanted more of each other and more life. We were adding on a baby to the house of our love. Like a sunroom, but made of wonder and fear and time and denial. It was the future. We pictured ourselves living there. All the imaginary firsts and the world going on as if it weren't already too late. It wasn't really as if the baby died. It wasn't even a baby, really. Not yet. I don't even like to use the word and wish there were a good alternative. It was more like the future died. It became part of the past.

Time inside of time. Things inside of things. The crow inside of me. The mouse in the belly of the trout. The belly of the girl on the golf course. Things that ache. Real things and unreal things. It is pointless to wish I had the hunger back instead of this endless grief.

In the morning, in the low river fog, there are two white horses. I think of the golf course and the white bodies of the girl and boy. I think maybe the horses are a dream, a hallucination, a consolation. Meaning. But then one horse climbs on top of the other. Its hooves are clumsy and inadequate. Its stiff penis is straight and thick as a rolling pin. Its bulk and desperation are absurd. When it is over, the horses stand next to each other grazing and flicking their tangled tails like nothing happened. They are beautiful, but they are just horses. "Huh," I say. And they both lift their heads to look at me and pause mid-chew. I wonder if they wonder what I am. They blink and puff white clouds of breath from their big warm nostrils. Finally one resumes chewing and then the other does.

Up ahead, the road doglegs sharply south and then west again, and just the way an eddy at the bend in a river traps leaves and dead fish and snakes and trash, at this bend in the road there is a blue-tarped gyre of trailers, Blue Bird school busses, reefers and boxcars, algae-streaked motor-homes and mildewed park models, all rafted together and piled in between with the rusted frames and mossy shells of cars and trucks. Smudgy spires of damp smoke, cooked meat, shit, urine, song and the sound of dogs barking ripple thinly up into the afternoon. Here is the apocalypse. Here are the living.

I think of leaving the road to avoid them. I think of waiting for dark. Of passing through their sleep like a spider. Why did I run from the old woman in the woods?

The sky is low and charged with snow that has not yet begun to fall. A flock of starlings keeps lifting off and landing, lifting off and landing. The sound of their wings all at once is soft and explosive. A hundred feathered concussions.

Before I can decide what to do, there is movement at the edge of the gyre. One two three four five of the living come out onto the road. I touch the stone in my cheek with my tongue.

—

I picture us as the crow would see us. From above. Flying. Which is how it exists inside me now. We are like the characters from the weekday matinee movie meeting for a showdown in the empty road. Stranger and townsfolk. Our shadows stretch long. The nervous strum of a Spanish guitar and one lonely trumpet.

They walk abreast. They advance. They close the distance between us.

With them, running ahead, there are the dogs, but even the bravest stops short. A heeler type. It makes snorting barks. It looks at me sideways. "Good dog," I say, and it howls a high, tight rebuff, keeping that one eye on me the whole time. "Okay," I say and I don't change my pace and at the last possible moment it turns and trots ahead of me back toward its people.

Even as they get closer, it is difficult to discern age or sex. Emaciated and dirty, they are just large or small, bearded or not. I can see the tension coiled in their bodies. The readiness. I can see they have a plan before I know what it is.

If there is a signal, an order, I miss it. They break into a run, rushing toward me and outward at the same time. Two of them dash to the shoulders of the road, unfurling something between them I momentarily expect to be a banner, as if they were only pretending to be extras from a spaghetti western but really they are a ragtag group of guerilla activists determined to confront this existential threat with the overwhelming force of a clear message. End The Zombie Apocalypse Now.

But of course it is a long, makeshift net. A net made of nets—volleyball nets, tennis nets, fishing nets sewn together with laundry line and bailing twine. They encircle me, close around me. Their actions are so choreographed and practiced, I think of a drill team. I feel like a participant in their performance.

Flash mob, protest, Clint Eastwood chewing on a skinny cheroot—it is all mixed into the moment the edge of the net draws tight across my ankles and sweeps me from my feet. A grunting sound comes out of me when I hit the pavement. They move fast and efficiently. They roll me up in the net like a badminton set being put away for winter so I can't move my arm or legs. I loved badminton.

They say nothing but "one, two, three" when they hoist me up. I swing between them as they walk. I am face down, which would be uncomfortable if I were alive, but as it is, is somewhat enjoyable. When was the last time I was carried? Was I seven? eight? I can see little more than the grey pavement and occasionally one dog or another as it darts in and back.

As we enter the gyre, we turn off the paved road and wind along branching paths. We seem to go on and on and I think this place must be much bigger than it appeared from the outside or else we are going in circles, doubling back. The paths are narrow and crowded on each side by a berm of human artifacts—I glimpse hubcaps, a Christmas tree stand, parts of tools, parts of machines, an old green garden hose, a car battery.

The path opens out into a clear space where the dirt is packed and oily looking. I can hear the waiting crowd. Their voices, low and tense, blend into a drone that reminds me of the chattering teeth of the hotel guests assembled on the roof for Marguerite's immolation.

If they were to burn me, would I find myself back in the plantation with the baseball team? If they cut me into little parts and bury me in separate holes, will that be that? Will I still think of you? Will my loss be multiplied or divided? I think of my arm and Janice 2's pinkie and Mitchem's penis and Marguerite's breasts and the baby. How small or altered or distant must a part of us be before it stops being a part of us? Does it ever? Is my cremated arm still sending me signals even now?

They set me down and the crowd closes in to get a look. They lean in and over. Their faces are full of fascination. Not for me, I think, but for their own fear. They take the measure of it, play it out, test it.

This is as close as I've been to the living since I killed the girl on the golf course and I look for the hunger. Perhaps somewhere in my body there sleeps a single sharp twinge. Like the sluggish winter wasps we sometimes accidentally brought inside with the firewood. Awakened by the warmth of the house, they would lumber through the air, stumble toward any light. We never killed them outright. I'd trap them in a glass, my heart racing, careful not to pinch a leg. You'd open the door for me and I'd fling them into the unsurvivable cold. What was so virtuous about that?

I do not find the hunger in me. But I can see it in the crowd. What is the difference between their hunger and mine? Is hunger, is rage, the attachment to one's own form? Is grief surrender?

I feel the space in my chest. I feel the stone in my cheek. I realize I am the winter wasp.

The crowd parts to let someone through. She is short and wide. She wears insulated Carhartt coveralls, the cuffs of the sleeves and legs cut off to fit, the thighs stained dark and slick, knees patched and repatched. She has bangs cut almost up to her hairline and long, thick braids. Her hair is the same butternut color as the Carhartts. Her skin, too. Sun-leathery and slightly jaundiced. She bends over me and her braids swing close to my face. Careless. If I were still as I was, as they imagine I am, I would lunge at the frizzling ends and pull her off balance and bite off her gourd nose.

She inspects me closely and without the same fear as the others, or with the same fear, but managed, consolidated into an air of leadership. Her eyes slide across my surface. She does not look at me so much as looks me over. It is an appraisal.

"Get it up," says Carhartt. The guerilla drill-team townsfolk step forward again and work to unfurl me from the net. They flip me over and over, realize they've gone the wrong way, flip me back, tug and wrestle with the tangled lines. It is awkward. I feel almost apologetic. I stay stiff to make their work easier. A button of my cardigan gets caught and springs off. I see it shoot away underfoot. It makes me a little sad.

The crowd grows silent and draws into itself as the last of the net is pulled away. Should I make a break for it? Could I even pretend to feel the old rage? I am held down and trussed up like a Christmas tree being made ready to take home on top of the family station wagon. They stand me up and hold me there—hold me steady and hold me captive, ready for the fight that I don't have in me.

I've never been good at estimating crowd size, but I'd say there must be a hundred or more people gathered. Around the perimeter of the clearing are tall crosses, planted crookedly at uneven intervals. The tallest is probably twenty feet tall. A few crosses are empty, but on most of them a decapitated body has been hoisted up, its head slung from the stub of its neck in the kind of mesh produce bag onions or tangerines used to come in. Some of the bodies are alert. They twitch and jerk at the end of their rope. Inside their mesh bags, turned this way and that, their eyes are restless, their teeth chatter, they chew their own tongues. But some of the bodies and heads appear lifeless. That is, dead. They are in various states of decay.

Do they punish everyone the same way here in the gyre—living or undead, off with your head—or were these dead once undead? I feel something like excitement. Fear? Hope? What in me wants to persist if there is no life to extend, no hunger to feed? What in me wants to die?

Finally the snow begins to fall. Small flakes, so slow and so few that it is possible to pick one out and follow it to the ground.

Carhartt steps forward. She walks all the way around me and my guards. The crowd waits, silent. She stops before me. All of her features are bunched together in the middle of her wide face like essential condiments at the center of a round table. Her eyes are blue and startling in contrast with her yellowbrownness. Clear and inscrutable. We look at each other. We meet in the space of our uncanny divide. I say, "None of this is real." Her eyes flick into a different kind of focus. Recognition. I feel a quiver somewhere not quite inside of me, goosebumps raised on a skin just outside of my skin. Her lips twitch around the thought she is thinking, the unthinkable, unsayable. "Well," I say, "some of it is real." She steps back from me. She reaches a hand straight out and to the side, palm up, decisive. A ruling. Someone steps forward and places in it the handle of a machete.

"Kneel," she says to me. She points with the machete at the ground. The guards push down on my shoulders. I fall to my knees and forward and they jerk my body back upright by the rope. Carhartt holds the machete just above the fold of my shirt collar, its blade just brushing my neck. She squints, marking a mental line where she will make the cut.

She plants her feet, winds up, and swings hard. The edge is keen and there is good follow-through on her stroke. My head hesitates for just a blink then topples sideways to the ground.

It lands with a thunk. I am not sure where I experience the sound—in my head or in my body. It seems both to come from me and near me at the same time. It is dark until I think to open my eyes, which I must have closed to receive the blow. The snow rushes slowly down at me from the white sky.

I open my mouth to say something, but I can't think what. I make a sound that is like the squiggly line you draw to get the ink to flow from a ball point pen. Warbling and a little too forceful.

I look up at my body kneeling there. Headless, one-armed, bound in rope. It is not like seeing myself in a mirror or even in a photograph. I am not strange to myself and at the same time I am new and fascinating. A friend I've had for years and suddenly fallen in love with. My first impulse is to touch my own cheek. Snowflakes land sharp and gently on my skin.

I look up at Carhartt, who is looking down at my body. The falling falling falling snow makes her seem to rise. I say, "I'm both."

It is decided that I should be hung upside down by my ankles since my missing arm makes it impossible to secure the lines around my chest. At some point my head is bagged up. I am unclear on the details, the sequence. The dislocation of sensation, the strangeness of being in two places at once, of being upside down and right side up at the same time, the dispassionate snow, the surrendering of my body's weight, it all gives me the feeling that I have stood up too fast—a swimming dizziness that does not subside. The snow continues to fall. I'm hoisted up the cross with my head slung over my feet. Carhartt says a few words. The crowd disperses. Darkness comes. Eventually there is no sound from the gyre. Sleep. Dream. I twist ever so slightly on my rope. My own head bump bumps lightly against my knees. The snow comes heavier. Each flake ticks as it lands in the silence. *Tick. Tick. Tick. Tick.* A vast timeless stippling.

In the morning, the world is white and still. The snow has stopped. The dizziness has stopped. My head is upright in its bag and faces away from my body, which seems lucky. I look around as far as I can in every direction, roll my eyes to find the limits of my view. I close one eye then the other, note the slight jog left right left right as I toggle between them.

I feel almost peaceful.

Blanketed in snow, its grime concealed, its makeshiftness smoothed, the gyre's order and form are plain. Concentric rings of shelters and paths radiate out from the central clearing. A miniature medieval city state surrounded by perfectly white fields surrounded by the leafless filigree of lowland alders and maples surrounded by the darker, flocked forest of firs and pines and cedars rising to the hill's crenelated ridge surrounded by clouds so low they catch in the ragged tops of trees.

I wonder what direction I am facing, if beyond those hills is the ocean, the dunes, the memory of you.

Not so bad to stay here forever, or for as long as passes for forever, until perhaps I die.

—

I grow accustomed to the feeling of hanging upside down while seeing the world right side up. This is how it is now. It snows on and off for what might be a week or months. The clouds never lift enough to show the sun or the moon. The sky is thick and motionless. It is either light or dark. There is no east or west.

On our crosses, we keep to ourselves. We look off in different directions, our heads turned one way or another. There are twelve of us. The hours of a clock with no hands. Meaningless. No one says anything, whether because the distance between us is not conducive to conversation or because we have nothing to say. I move the white stone from one cheek to the other. It feels like an important secret. A blade baked into a cake.

Every day the living make their dirty tracks and every day they are covered over. Smoke from their cook fires hangs uncertainly above the gyre. We twist untended.

The snowflakes are soft and slow as feathers thickening the air, or they are tiny and sharp, each on its own path. It is the same with the people who pass through the clearing. Sometimes a pair, sometimes alone. Bundled against the cold, they hurry on errands or seem almost aimless. They sometimes glance up at us. If they stop too long, it makes the other undead restless. They strain on their tethers, wriggle in their ropes, causing little flurries of snow to drop from their clothes and the crosstrees of their crosses. Their hands flutter and grasp.

The children—there are children here—throw snowballs at us. This inevitably breaks down into snowball fights with each other. One day they make a snowman in the center of the clearing and then cut off its head. They use the head to make a new snowman, then cut off its head, too. And so on until this gets boring and they leave. The headless snowmen stand together in the clearing, the last unused head lying on the trampled ground between them.

One night the wind comes up. It is sudden and strong and warm. I swing out from my cross. My head bumps and spins in its bag. It blows hard for I don't know how long and then drops again as abruptly as it started. There is a deep, sweet-smelling silence and then the rain begins.

The snow shrinks back fast over the coming days, reduced to stubborn icy paths in high traffic areas and muddy islands in the margins. The headless snowmen become a collection of cone-shaped pillars stained yellow where dogs have lifted a leg on their way by, then shapeless mounds, then they are gone. The clearing is churned into a mud puddle and boards are laid down to make paths across it.

I am losing days to seasons until one evening the old woman from the woods appears at the edge of the clearing. She wears the same dark duster, the mushroom cap hat. She is a dusky shadow in the dusk. She has her walking stick and her satchel across her chest. She stands as if at a threshold. She looks up at the cross that is at nine o'clock, third from mine clockwise. She is about to step forward when someone arrives at the clearing from another path. She turns quickly and is gone before they see her.

Two days later, she returns early in the morning. Just light enough for me to be able to recognize her. She hobbles quickly across the clearing and steps off the boardwalk path to stand at Nine o'clock's cross. She gazes up silently as if the young woman dangling there is Jesus himself hanging over an altar. Nine o'clock's hair is pressed into a dark, wet mat inside her onion bag. Her flowered blouse is threadbare and torn as a flag left up through every weather so you can see her aqua colored lace bra. She has on skinny jeans that pinch a roll of belly up over their low waist. The old woman says something, maybe a name, and Nine o'clock jerks like someone startled from sleep. The old woman talks to her in the same way she talked to the child in the shed. As if she's updating a coma patient on recent events. She keeps her voice low and it is hard for me to make out what she says. I am torn between straining to hear every word and pretending I can't hear anything at all. It seems impolite to listen in, wrong even. Like opening a letter delivered to the wrong address and pretending that the "you" of the letter is really you.

You. You can be anyone.

Nine o'clock grows more and more agitated. She clacks her teeth and struggles against her bindings. It rouses the others and they begin to stir. Twelve o'clock, Two o'clock. The old woman from the woods glances around the clearing nervously, not worried about us, it seems, but about any attention we might draw. "Well. Better go," I hear her say. She kisses the tips of her fingers and transfers the kiss to Nine o'clock's cross. "Love you," she says. Nine o'clock jerks and twists at the end of her rope, snaps her teeth and snarls. It rouses Five o'clock, who moans loudly. The old woman looks up at him as she turns to go and spots me looking down at her. I see her recognition. She stumbles and lets go of her walking stick to break her fall with her one good hand. I lurch forward as if I could catch her. She grunts as she lands hard against the edge of the boardwalk. Her hat comes off. She is still. She looks like a large duffle bag. The rain rolls off her duster. There is movement in the gyre. Someone has heard us. They will come. "They are coming," I say. I'm afraid I will swallow the stone or it will drop from my mouth. "Get up," I say. She rolls onto her side and looks up at me.

"Are you alive?" she says.

"Hurry," I say.

She struggles to kneel, then to stand, planting her walking stick in the mud and hauling herself up. She is covered in mud. Bent in pain. She turns to leave the way she came. "Not that way," I say.

She changes course, hurries toward one of the other entrances to the clearing. Her hat lies on the ground and I would say something about it but there isn't time. She is gone by the time they arrive in the clearing.

The rain stops. The clouds pull back like a pool cover, revealing the sky that has been there all along. Bright blue and bottomless. The moon floats there round and pale as a jellyfish. I feel the warmth of the sun rising behind me. The shadow of my cross stretches across the clearing. Our clock begins to tell time.

Sundial. Compass. Time and space.

Every day the birds begin to sing while it is still dark. Every day the sun sets a little farther north along the low ridge of the hills. The sky turns orange then pink then purple. The names of the stars and planets, the constellations, are not among the names I've forgotten. I never knew them. The nights are shorter and shorter. In the morning there is frost on the fields, on the tarps and moss-covered roofs of the hovels, on me.

I often imagine I am hearing the ocean. Is that the same as hearing it? I remember reading about a study that showed an increase in the body temperature of participants who were instructed to imagine they were sitting beside a crackling fire. Instructed to imagine. Imagine that. Imagine this.

The mud dries hard and the boardwalks are removed. I expect the old woman to return, but she doesn't until I stop thinking about it. Then one night when I am listening to the frogs, there she is, hobbling around the edge of the clearing. She stops at my cross and stands there looking up at me. She is blue in the moonlight.

"Pssst," she says.

I don't know what the right response is. I tuck the stone safely in the pocket of my cheek. "Pssst," I say back.

"Are you alive?" she says. She enunciates each word with the care of a space explorer enacting the procedure for establishing contact with an alien life form.

"No," I say.

"What are you?" she says, moving through the script. She is just loud enough that I can hear her over the galactic static of the peepers and throaty bullfrogs.

"I'm trying to get to the ocean," I say. I find myself speaking in the same odd way. It lends an urgency to the words that I had forgotten I feel.

She pauses. "Why aren't you like the others?" she says.

It is such an important question. Why am I. Am I not?

"Why aren't you?" I say.

She seems to sag down. Surrender. I think maybe she is crying. She looks over at Nine o'clock hanging on her cross. She looks back at me. Finally she says, not in the same way, giving up on first-contact protocol, "What's at the ocean?"

What is at the ocean. What is at the ocean.

"I think there just has to be somewhere I'm going," I say.

She is quiet for a long time. Then she says more to herself than to me, "Maybe you're just clever and I'm more stupid than I knew." She shrugs. She nods. Then she says, now in the voice you use to keep from startling someone off the window ledge you're rescuing them from, "I'm going to let you down from there."

She goes to the base of my cross and I can't see what she is doing, but I feel the line moving and suddenly I am not ready, to go on, to lose more. I look around at the other hours of the clock, at the moonlit gyre and fields, at the dome of the sky rising from the distant ridge, at the stars. Take a picture with your mind, my mother used to say. Then I am being lowered down and the ground seems to rise up under me like the curved back of a living, breathing thing. I feel as if I could slide off, as if my head will tumble away, and I am only barely aware of the old woman working the knots that bind me and pulling away the rope. When she's got my ankles free she says, "Can you stand?" I don't know. My feet are giant helium balloons that will lift me up and carry me away upside down. She picks up my head in its bag and slings it across her chest with her satchel. I think of the gun, the tourniquet, the wooden spoon. She has a clean smoky smell. I feel her hand close around my wrist and I grasp hers in return. She pulls me up. The world spins and I lurch to the side. She grips my arm in hers and I picture us floating up over the fields linked arm in arm. "We have to hurry," she says, her voice close now, reassuring and firm. I stumble blindly and nearly pull us down. She tucks her arm firmly around my waist. She pulls me forward and keeps me on my feet.

"What about Nine o'clock?" I say, my voice muffled in the folds of her duster. She doesn't respond. "Nine o'clock, Nine o'clock," I say, not sure whether she can't hear me or can't make sense of me. I wonder if this is how the crow felt, and at the thought of its feathered body I begin to cry. I try not to wonder how this is possible or if I am imagining it because I don't want it to stop even if it isn't really happening. Maybe I'm crying from being so close to her. Maybe because she rescued me. Saw me.

I am crying as we stagger through the gyre and when we come out onto the road and still as we cut across the field along an old fenceline, clearing a path of silence through the peepers that slowly closes up behind us. I cry as I get used to the bump and roll of her hip and the flap of her empty sleeve. I lift my feet high with every step to keep from tripping and lean into the old woman to steady myself. She leans back on me and I think she must have left her walking stick behind in the clearing. I am still crying when we reach the edge of the woods and still as we move uphill through alders and maples into the darker, towering silence of the evergreens.

At first I feel it in my head, the crying, a pressure and a release. Like a realization. Then it is more like a rend in my stomach. It becomes possible to cry without focusing on it.

I cry as we start downhill again following an old logging road, and as we come to the river and the railroad tracks. I cry at the sound of the river and how much higher it is running now with winter runoff. I cry while I learn the rhythm of crossties and ballast underfoot. We are not hurrying any-more. I don't need as much assistance, but the old woman keeps ahold of my arm. I think now it is more for her than for me. We are like convalescent and nurse, but I'm not sure who is who.

I am crying as the night thins and the birds begin to call high up in the branches. I am crying while I wonder if we are going to the shed where she keeps the child, if she is planning to shut me in with him, if she thinks perhaps he'll like the taste of me. Or maybe I'll be his companion.

I am crying even as I think about the crying. I think, this is what remains after the swarm. I think, this is emptiness itself. I think it is more the emptiness of a church than the emptiness of an empty home. Big and high-ceilinged and nothing in it belongs only to me. And when I think this, I feel a stab of fear at the sadness yet to come and I stop crying.

We leave the tracks and I think we must be at the shed except I do not hear the river. We keep going and when the sun slants through the trees behind us I realize we've gone west not east. Finally we stop. "Sit here," the old woman says, and guides me to a fallen tree grown over with moss and ferns. It is soft and cool. She unslings my head from across her chest and props it up at the base of a nearby tree so that I am facing myself. She settles next to me with a groan and massages her knees. I look at us sitting there side by side. Mostly at me. This third person perspective on myself is disconcerting.

I run my fingers absently through the moss covering our log, feeling its spongy, springy dampness with my fingers and noticing from my position on the ground that it is the same color as my sweater. I don't look as bad as you'd think after a winter hanging upside down outside. Not even that rumpled. Though my white sneakers are soaked through and covered in dirt from our trek and my pants are wet up to the knees from dew, the wool darker and heavy.

The old woman reaches into her satchel and pulls out a green plastic bottle. The kind that 7-Up or Mountain Dew came in. The label is gone. She holds it between her knees and untwists the cap. I half expect it to fizz over. She hesitates and offers it to me. "Water?" she says. "No thank you," I say. I raise my hand to decline. We are both a little surprised by the dislocated gesture. She takes a long swig from the bottle and it is funny to remember needing to drink, to keep the body going, to tend to a need rather than a compulsion.

"Is it your child in the shed?" I ask.

"Grandson," she says.

"I thought you were taking me there," I say.

She recaps the bottle and puts it back in her satchel, rummages around and takes out a little cloth bundle of something like trail mix. I wonder what all she has in there. I think of the gun. I think of her biting down on the wooden spoon. I want to tell her that she doesn't have to feed the boy. That maybe she shouldn't. But you can't tell other people how to parent, especially when you don't have kids yourself.

"I know it makes no difference," she says. "What I give him." Did I say my thought out loud? "I always spoiled him. Couldn't help it. Making up for what I did wrong with his mother, maybe. Going too far the other way." She looks up into the trees. Their leaves are new and tender and lit with pale sky.

"Maybe we have to go too far," I say.

"Too far," she says. "Too late. We learn too late. Too late is how we learn." She holds up the stub of her arm and wags the empty sleeve back and forth. I lift the cuff of my loose sleeve with my remaining hand and wave it at her. She laughs. And then I laugh. It surprises us both and we laugh again. It is so close to crying I'm afraid I won't be able to stop, but it isn't the same. "Oh, lordy," she says. "Lordy, lordy." She keeps saying it as she bundles the trail mix back up and tucks it in her satchel. "Lordy, lordy, oh lordy, lordy, lordy."

She heaves herself up and limps stiffly over to my head. "Ooh, lordy, lordy. Old knees, you old knees." She picks up my head and brings it back to me on the log. "Stand up," she says. She slings the lanyard across my chest. I think of a beauty contestant receiving her sash. Miss Congeniality. Miss America. I feel for my head and tilt it inside the mesh sack so it is roughly upright and facing forward at my side. I feel my fingers on my face. I feel my face with my fingers. Even severed, it is impossible to tell one sensation from the other. I adjust where the line hits the stub of my neck, pulling up the collar of my shirt and folding it over.

I stand up from the log. Take a few steps. Like I'm trying on a pair of shoes. I wander around, trying to get the hang of it. When I look where I'm stepping I stumble, the ground farther away than it appears. I find it works better to hold my head in the crook of my arm, pivoting and bending forward or back to look where I want.

The old woman hunts around for a new walking stick. She picks up fallen branches, tries them for length, rejects them. I think I need my own stick. A stake.

We move among the silent trees, searching the ferns and duff of last fall's leaves. It is like when I was a horse. Eventually I find a good straight branch, the right thickness, the right length, still strong.

The old woman sits on the log using a knife she takes from her satchel to whittle away the twigs and rough bark from the branch she finds for herself, smoothing out a comfortable grip at the right height. She does the same for mine and sharpens both ends to points, one for my head and one to plant in the ground when I need to free my hand.

We take my head out of the sack and prop it upside down at a good angle. I hold it steady and on the count of three the old woman plunges the stake into it with a single unflinching grunt. The point goes true through the soft triangle of my throat and into the firm mud of my brain. She uses a rock to knock it the rest of the way in until the point taps the inside of my skull.

I tilt the stake upright and stand with it in my grip. The length is perfect, my head just above shoulder height. I pivot it one way, the other. Realize I can spin it all the way around to see behind me. There is the old woman. She shakes her head. "Lordy, lordy," she says.

"Lordy, lordy," I say.

And then it is time to part ways.

"Head downhill," the old woman says, "and eventually you'll come to the road. We're past the bridge where they have scouts. What's after that I don't know."

I tell her about the plantation. About the baseball team. I don't promise anything. I don't know if there is an answer there for her grandson. I don't mention the gazebo or the hole. I tell her to ask for Marguerite. I wish I could tell her to say I sent her. To send my regards. It is the first time I've missed my name.

There's no real goodbye. We just turn from each other.

PART 7

Then there is a loneliness that roams. No rocking can hold it down. It is alive, on its own. A dry and spreading thing that makes the sound of one's own feet going seem to come from a far-off place.

— Toni Morrison

THE ROAD GOES UP AND down with the shape of the land. I go up and down with the road. My head goes up and down atop the stake, a little swoop, dip, rise, not quite in time with my steps. Syncopated. Always a little out front, my body falling behind and catching up.

I am getting a feel for this new arrangement of myself. The balance of my head on its stake, the balance of my body without a head, the way some things occur first to my body and some to my head.

Remember the therapist who talked about congruence? It was a good thing to be congruent with oneself. Sitting on her neutral couch, I pictured myself as two lines not touching, running indefinitely through a landscape, bumping up perfectly over rocks and tracing the outlines of trees, always equidistant from each other and from the surface of solid things. Myself running in a line beside myself.

Even then I wondered, Wouldn't it be better to be *in* ` congruent? To have the chance of meeting myself if only for a fleeting moment?

There is a much better chance of that now.

Shifts in pace, duration, perspective.

I pass through more empty towns. A logging town with yarded logs rotting in their piles. An oyster town with dirty white mountains of oyster shells. A cranberry town with gorse and alders coming up in the bogs.

I meet no one. Living or dead.

After a long time I come suddenly to the end. The road would continue if it could, but there is no more land. The pavement falls unceremoniously away, the dashed yellow line of the lane divider broken off. The thought hangs there unfinished.

...

No beach pines. No dune grass. No dunes. No sign that we were ever here. No here where we ever were.

I step down from the world's crumbling edge. It is winter warm, like that other day. The air clear and cold, the sun bright and hot. The tide is far out. The line of the surf a mile or more away. The sand is rippled like the roof of a cat's mouth and rises impossibly up to the thin, mirage shimmer of breakers in the distance. There are pools and rivers of tidal water blue as the sky. Bluer, even.

I walk out onto the beach. The sand is loose below its wind-shaped skin. It falls away from my steps and fills my shoes. Here and there, bleached silver and half buried, are massive driftwood snags washed from this shore or some other beyond the planet's curve.

I plant the end of my stake in the sand, twisting it in firmly and turning it so I face the ocean. I take off my sneakers and set them in the lee of a driftwood tree whose useless roots fan up into the sky. I pull off my socks and stuff one in each shoe. The sand is warm on the surface and cold just beneath. I roll up the cuffs of my nice pants. I take off my green cardigan and hang it from a twisting silver root.

I am going to take my head, then I change my mind. Or maybe it is something else I change. I set off across the beach without myself.

I watch me walk away, my empty sleeve flapping in the empty day.

I am two places at once. I am walking in the direction I am seeing myself walk.

I look smaller and smaller.

I feel wider and wider.

Where I walk, the sand is wet. In some places it is firm and strange on the soles of my feet, in others loose and soupy.

From where I watch, the sand is dry. It hisses when the wind blows.

I used to imagine how it would be after you died. The way my days would go. It wasn't bad. I would have had so much in having you and would have lost so much in losing you that I would no longer want anything. There would be more time. I pictured myself moving through the quiet house. I saw myself in the garden—my face, my back, my hands changed by not saying anything to anyone day after day. I saw the sheets I would wash and hang out to dry and fold and put away. The short showers I would take. The short hair I would have. I would put on the same clothes every morning and hang them on a hook every night. I was an old woman who looked like an old man. When I would leave the house, I would take my solitariness with me. I would roll down the grocery store aisles neither fast nor slow and put only a few items in my cart, not worrying about the cost of the cheese and sometimes buying eight of the same frozen meal. I would make no chitchat with clerks or retired neighbors. Sometimes I might accept a dinner invitation, and I would bring a gift for the host (sometimes a young couple new to the block, sometimes an old friend who had known me with you), but it would be a relief to everyone when I left without fail at exactly eight-thirty making no excuses.

I realize now that when I was playing these silent movies of life after our life, you were still there. You were sitting with me, the two of us alone in the theater, still together. This sadness is not an empty church and not an empty house. It is the whole empty world and I am in it and it is in me.

—

By now I am an uncertain speck against the shifting horizon and I keep going. The sound of the surf is as far away as you. The surge of ions pushed before the breakers is just as close. It fills my shirt, my skin, and I think maybe I will see me tumble up into the sky empty as a pillowcase plucked by the wind from a laundry line.

The first wave curves cold across my ankles. Is this where I have been going?

I wanted to grieve while I still had the solace of you.

The next wave swells cold around my legs and sucks the sand from under my feet as it recedes. I am any broken shell.

The end of the world happens so quietly. Things as large as glaciers are so quiet.

The next wave and the next. The next and the next. I continue until I feel the tug of the current. I lie back and the water draws me out, draws me under. Cold cold. I am a ribbon of kelp.

I look up and there is the moon. Pale disc in the blue. It is not quite whole. Disappearing at last.

The tide comes fast across the flat shore. I hear it coming.

I am carried out. One arm. No head. An empty space below my heart.

At the edge of the surf, a flock of small, flashing v-winged birds flies south to north. Later they return and settle fast-legged and twittering on the wet sand. Or maybe it is some other flock.

Everything moves in the same way. One bird. One thousand. The ocean. The moon. The sky comes all the way down to the water. I am somewhere below.

—

The sun sets. I watch it go. It sinks very quickly and I'm not ready for it to be gone. Just before it goes, it slows. The last moment is long and sudden. The next moment is vast and loud. The sky and the waves. Then just after everything is over, it isn't. The curved red bite of the sun's edge emerges again below the horizon because the horizon is not the horizon after all but only a band of clouds. Between it and the sea, there is a gap of sky, narrow and pearl pale.

It is as if I am watching from here as the sun rises on some other continent, watching the beginning of some other person's day on the far side of a world I have misunderstood until this moment, thinking the sky is overhead, that I know rise from set, beginning from end.

At one point the sun is sinking both in and out of view and seems to not be sinking at all, but standing still. By the time it finally sets, I expect to see it again. I wait, but this time it is really gone.

The tide goes out. The tide comes in. The tide goes out. The tide comes in. My body does not return to me. The green sweater blows away. The sand covers my shoes. There is less and less moon, then there is more again, but still I am alone.

A crow flies low and lifts at the last minute to light in the roots of the driftwood tree.

Somewhere in the ocean I move my hand to my silent heart.

For a while the crow pretends I am not here, but finally it meets my eyes, briefly, then turns its back. When it turns to me again, I say, "Are you my crow?"

Would I know you now?

It caws four times. Its whole body bobs up and down with each caw.

"I can't understand you anymore," I say. Not that I ever could.

It caws again four times.

"I don't have anything but my eyes," I say. "You can take my eyes."

It hops to a new perch, wipes both sides of its beak on its foot and caws again.

I remember the white stone I have gotten so used to not swallowing.

"Would you like this stone?" I say. I spit it as far as I can. It makes a little divot in the sand where it lands. I have kept it tucked in my cheek all this time and it feels good to have it gone. The crow looks at it there in the sand, my sadness or my hope. Tilts its head. Ruffles its wings. Hops again to a new perch. Tilts its head the other way. It flaps down to the sand near the stone. Jumps back theatrically. Walk-skips forward again.

The crow picks up the stone in its beak and flaps a little ways off. It holds the stone steady between its feet and pecks at it. This way. Then that way. It tries various angles. Finally it takes it up and flies away.

When you have arrived at the thing itself, then all you can do is compare it to something else you don't understand. A rock. A crow. The only things that remain themselves are the ones you can never reach. The things that are too big or too far away or move too slowly to detect. Smooth. Feathered. Loved. Already lost. They will always be only what they really are, and you will never know what name to call out to them.

—

I am in the ocean. I am on the shore. I am trying to remember or to see.

The space between me and me is you. This is a mystery.

NOTES ON EPIGRAPHS

ACKNOWLEDGMENTS

Thank you to the place in which my work is rooted, and to all its creatures.

To the artists and writers whose accumulated and continuing work contributed to my endeavor.

To the people who make up New Directions, Fitzcarraldo and Giramondo.

To the friends who gave essential time, space, insight, encouragement and companionship:

Jennifer Calkins, Natalie Smith, Carlos Sirah, Stephanie Kaye, Lenny Kaye, Dawn McCarra Bass, Rick Simonson, Bradley Huson, Greg Rogers, Lisa Sweet, Susan Christian, the Water Closet and Sister Mary Pruitt.

Thanks to my brother, who went first.

And thank you to M Freeman. More than anything, more than ever.

New Directions Paperbooks — a partial listing

Kaouther Adimi, Our Riches

Adonis, Songs of Mihyar the Damascene

César Aira, Ghosts
An Episode in the Life of a Landscape Painter

Will Alexander, Refractive Africa

Osama Alomar, The Teeth of the Comb

Guillaume Apollinaire, Selected Writings

Jessica Au, Cold Enough for Snow

Paul Auster, The Red Notebook

Ingeborg Bachmann, Malina

Honoré de Balzac, Colonel Chabert

Djuna Barnes, Nightwood

Charles Baudelaire, The Flowers of Evil*

Bei Dao, City Gate, Open Up

Mei-Mei Berssenbrugge, Empathy

Max Blecher, Adventures in Immediate Irreality

Roberto Bolaño, By Night in Chile
Distant Star

Jorge Luis Borges, Labyrinths
Seven Nights

Beatriz Bracher, Antonio

Coral Bracho, Firefly Under the Tongue*

Kamau Brathwaite, Ancestors

Basil Bunting, Complete Poems

Anne Carson, Glass, Irony & God
Norma Jeane Baker of Troy

Horacio Castellanos Moya, Senselessness

Camilo José Cela, Mazurka for Two Dead Men

Louis-Ferdinand Céline
Death on the Installment Plan
Journey to the End of the Night

Rafael Chirbes, Cremation

Inger Christensen, alphabet

Julio Cortázar, Cronopios & Famas

Jonathan Creasy (ed.), Black Mountain Poems

Robert Creeley, If I Were Writing This

Guy Davenport, 7 Greeks

Amparo Davila, The Houseguest

Osamu Dazai, No Longer Human
The Setting Sun

H.D., Selected Poems

Helen DeWitt, The Last Samurai
Some Trick

Marcia Douglas
The Marvellous Equations of the Dread

Daša Drndić, EEG

Robert Duncan, Selected Poems

Eça de Queirós, The Maias

William Empson, 7 Types of Ambiguity

Mathias Énard, Compass

Shusaku Endo, Deep River

Jenny Erpenbeck, The End of Days
Go, Went, Gone

Lawrence Ferlinghetti
A Coney Island of the Mind

Thalia Field, Personhood

F. Scott Fitzgerald, The Crack-Up
On Booze

Emilio Fraia, Sevastopol

Jean Frémon, Now, Now, Louison

Rivka Galchen, Little Labors

Forrest Gander, Be With

Romain Gary, The Kites

Natalia Ginzburg, The Dry Heart
Happiness, as Such

Henry Green, Concluding

Felisberto Hernández, Piano Stories

Hermann Hesse, Siddhartha

Takashi Hiraide, The Guest Cat

Yoel Hoffmann, Moods

Susan Howe, My Emily Dickinson
Concordance

Bohumil Hrabal, I Served the King of England

Qurratulain Hyder, River of Fire

Sonallah Ibrahim, That Smell

Rachel Ingalls, Mrs. Caliban

Christopher Isherwood, The Berlin Stories

Fleur Jaeggy, Sweet Days of Discipline

Alfred Jarry, Ubu Roi

B.S. Johnson, House Mother Normal

James Joyce, Stephen Hero

Franz Kafka, Amerika: The Man Who Disappeared

Yasunari Kawabata, Dandelions

John Keene, Counternarratives

Heinrich von Kleist, Michael Kohlhaas

Alexander Kluge, Temple of the Scapegoat

Wolfgang Koeppen, Pigeons on the Grass

Taeko Kono, Toddler-Hunting

Laszlo Krasznahorkai, Satantango
Seiobo There Below

Ryszard Krynicki, Magnetic Point

Eka Kurniawan, Beauty Is a Wound

Mme. de Lafayette, The Princess of Clèves

Lautréamont, Maldoror

Siegfried Lenz, The German Lesson
Alexander Lernet-Holenia, Count Luna
Denise Levertov, Selected Poems
Li Po, Selected Poems
Clarice Lispector, The Hour of the Star
  The Passion According to G. H.
Federico García Lorca, Selected Poems*
Nathaniel Mackey, Splay Anthem
Xavier de Maistre, Voyage Around My Room
Stéphane Mallarmé, Selected Poetry and Prose*
Javier Marías, Your Face Tomorrow (3 volumes)
Adam Mars-Jones, Box Hill
Bernadette Mayer, Midwinter Day
Carson McCullers, The Member of the Wedding
Fernando Melchor, Hurricane Season
Thomas Merton, New Seeds of Contemplation
  The Way of Chuang Tzu
Henri Michaux, A Barbarian in Asia
Dunya Mikhail, The Beekeeper
Henry Miller, The Colossus of Maroussi
  Big Sur & the Oranges of Hieronymus Bosch
Yukio Mishima, Confessions of a Mask
  Death in Midsummer
Eugenio Montale, Selected Poems*
Vladimir Nabokov, Laughter in the Dark
  Nikolai Gogol
Pablo Neruda, The Captain's Verses*
  Love Poems*
Charles Olson, Selected Writings
George Oppen, New Collected Poems
Wilfred Owen, Collected Poems
Hiroko Oyamada, The Hole
José Emilio Pacheco, Battles in the Desert
Michael Palmer, Little Elegies for Sister Satan
Nicanor Parra, Antipoems*
Boris Pasternak, Safe Conduct
Octavio Paz, Poems of Octavio Paz
Victor Pelevin, Omon Ra
Georges Perec, Ellis Island
Alejandra Pizarnik
  Extracting the Stone of Madness
Ezra Pound, The Cantos
  New Selected Poems and Translations
Raymond Queneau, Exercises in Style
Qian Zhongshu, Fortress Besieged
Herbert Read, The Green Child
Kenneth Rexroth, Selected Poems
Keith Ridgway, A Shock

Rainer Maria Rilke
  Poems from the Book of Hours
Arthur Rimbaud, Illuminations*
  A Season in Hell and The Drunken Boat*
Evelio Rosero, The Armies
Fran Ross, Oreo
Joseph Roth, The Emperor's Tomb
Raymond Roussel, Locus Solus
Ihara Saikaku, The Life of an Amorous Woman
Nathalie Sarraute, Tropisms
Jean-Paul Sartre, Nausea
Judith Schalansky, An Inventory of Losses
Delmore Schwartz
  In Dreams Begin Responsibilities
W.G. Sebald, The Emigrants
  The Rings of Saturn
Anne Serre, The Governesses
Patti Smith, Woolgathering
Stevie Smith, Best Poems
  Novel on Yellow Paper
Gary Snyder, Turtle Island
Dag Solstad, Professor Andersen's Night
Muriel Spark, The Driver's Seat
Maria Stepanova, In Memory of Memory
Wislawa Szymborska, How to Start Writing
Antonio Tabucchi, Pereira Maintains
Junichiro Tanizaki, The Maids
Yoko Tawada, The Emissary
  Memoirs of a Polar Bear
Dylan Thomas, A Child's Christmas in Wales
  Collected Poems
Tomas Tranströmer, The Great Enigma
Leonid Tsypkin, Summer in Baden-Baden
Tu Fu, Selected Poems
Paul Valéry, Selected Writings
Enrique Vila-Matas, Bartleby & Co.
Elio Vittorini, Conversations in Sicily
Rosmarie Waldrop, The Nick of Time
Robert Walser, The Assistant
  The Tanners
Eliot Weinberger, An Elemental Thing
  The Ghosts of Birds
Nathanael West, The Day of the Locust
  Miss Lonelyhearts
Tennessee Williams, The Glass Menagerie
  A Streetcar Named Desire
William Carlos Williams, Selected Poems
Louis Zukofsky, "A"

*BILINGUAL EDITION

For a complete listing, request a free catalog from New Directions, 80 8th Avenue, New York, NY 10011
or visit us online at **ndbooks.com**